DRESSED TO FRILL

written by
Chloe Taylor

illustrated by
Nancy Zhang

Simon Spotlight
New York London Toronto Sydney New Delhi

JPF
Taylor

SIMON SPOTLIGHT
An imprint of Simon & Schuster Children's Publishing Division
1230 Avenue of the Americas, New York, New York 10020
First Simon Spotlight paperback edition June 2015
Copyright © 2015 by Simon and Schuster, Inc.
All rights reserved, including the right of reproduction in whole or in part in any form.
SIMON SPOTLIGHT and colophon are registered trademarks of Simon & Schuster, Inc.
For information about special discounts for bulk purchases, please contact Simon & Schuster Special Sales at 1-866-506-1949 or business@simonandschuster.com.
Text by Sarah Darer Littman
Designed by Laura Roode
Manufactured in the United States of America 0515 OFF
10 9 8 7 6 5 4 3 2 1
ISBN 978-1-4814-2931-3 (hc)
ISBN 978-1-4814-2930-6 (pbk)
ISBN 978-1-4814-2932-0 (eBook)
Library of Congress Catalog Card Number 2014959225

CHAPTER 1

Fired Up

I know you're not supposed to enjoy being "fired" from a job, but I've been all "fired up" with new ideas for outfits since getting kicked out as treasurer of the Fashion Fun Club. See the fruits of my labor (or of my firing?) in the sketch! Aunt Lulu said maybe the club was too much of a good thing. That sometimes you need to take a break and do something completely different (and for me, that means *not* sewing related), so your mind can wander to new and exciting creative places. It's also really nice to have time to do nothing at all!

That's why I love volunteering at the pet shelter. With all those adorable dogs and cats to walk and play with, you never know what's going to happen next. I always come away with more energy for my sewing projects.

We're starting the next elective in school soon. I'm excited to try industrial arts. I wonder if I can somehow figure out how to combine woodworking and fashion. But how would you sit down in a wooden dress? Hmm . . . will clearly have to give this a bit more thought. ☺

"I need your advice," Kate Mackey announced to her best friends, Zoey Webber, Priti Holbrooke, and Libby Flynn. "I'm thinking of giving Tyler another chance."

The girls were in their pajamas, lounging around

on Libby's bed. It was sleepover night at the Flynn house.

"What made you decide that?" Zoey asked. Kate had broken up with Tyler Landon, who'd had a crush on her, a few weeks earlier after only a few dates, partially due to Zoey's misguided attempts to help him woo her. Under Zoey's helpful advice (which turned out to be not so helpful after all!), Tyler had been behaving differently than usual because he'd thought it would make Kate like him.

"Well . . . we have a great time together when we volunteer at the food pantry," Kate said.

"Not to mention the fact that he's *super*cute," Priti observed.

Kate blushed. "Well, yes, there *is* that," she admitted. "But also he's promised just to be himself this time."

Now it was Zoey's turn to blush.

"I was only trying to help," she said for what must have been the umpteenth time since her matchmaking fiasco.

"I know," Kate said, smiling. "All is forgiven. . . . Really."

"Whew!" Zoey exhaled, relieved. "I'd hate to think I completely ruined everything."

"You guys seem to have a lot of fun when we're at the food pantry," Libby observed. She'd started volunteering there, in addition to her school community service at the pet shelter, so she had seen Kate and Tyler together.

"I'm glad you've decided to give Tyler another chance," Zoey told Kate. "What if I'd messed up the course of true love?"

"*True love?!*" Kate exclaimed. "Let's not go overboard. I just think he's nice. And funny."

"And supercute," Priti added.

"I guess," Kate mumbled, blushing a little.

"Well, since we've agreed that Tyler is supercute, can I show you something superexciting?" Libby asked.

"Yes, please!" Priti said.

Libby jumped off the bed and went to her desk.

"Look! Hot off the press!" she said, holding out an embossed card threaded with gold ribbon. "My Bat Mitzvah invitation. Isn't it cool?"

"It's beautiful!" Priti exclaimed.

"I love the gold ribbon," Zoey said. "It makes the lettering pop."

"And the gold lining inside the envelope matches the lettering and the ribbon," Kate observed. "So pretty!"

Libby climbed back onto the bed and sat cross-legged.

"A few years ago, I wasn't even sure I was going to have a Bat Mitzvah. Dad's Catholic and Mom's Jewish, but neither of them are that religious. We celebrate all the holidays, but more the traditions than the religious stuff," she explained.

"So what made you change your mind?" Zoey asked.

"My grandpa," Libby said. "He only just escaped the Holocaust as a young boy. In fact, his name wasn't Van Langen when he was born. But his parents hid him with non-Jewish neighbors when my great-grandparents were sent to a concentration camp. And then . . . Well, they didn't come back after the war, and he ended up adopting the name of the family who hid him and saved his life."

"That's so sad," Kate said. "He never saw his parents again?"

"Never," Libby said, shaking her head. "And he hardly ever talked about it until recently, when he said it would mean a lot to him if I had a Bat Mitzvah. So that's why I decided to do it. But it's *so much* work, which is the reason I haven't been around lately."

"I've never been to a Bat Mitzvah before," Zoey admitted. "What do you do? What do *we* do? And more to the point, what do we *wear*?"

The girls all laughed.

"Zoey always gets right down to the important questions," Priti said.

"Well, there'll be a service in the synagogue," Libby explained, then reached over to the bedside table and picked up some papers. "And I have to read a section of the Torah in Hebrew. I've been going to a tutor and practicing my Torah portion every night before I go to bed, and listening to tapes so I get the pronunciation right. See?"

Zoey looked at the unfamiliar alphabet. "It looks like Greek to me."

"Ha!" Libby said. "It felt like Greek to me when I first started. Except now that I've been studying it for a while, I can tell it's Hebrew, even though it's still hard to read."

"I can't believe how much work you have to do," Priti said. "It's really great that you're doing this for your grandpa."

"It's not just for him. It's become important to me too," Libby said. "But I also have to make a speech, which I'm really nervous about. On the plus side, I get to have a really fun party after the service."

"Party? Did you say party?" Priti perked up immediately.

"I've been to a Bar Mitzvah party before—it was really fun," Kate said. "They played lots of games, and the food was amazing."

"Yeah, Mom and I met with the caterers last week," Libby said. "The theme of my Bat Mitzvah is going to be 'Sweet,' so needless to say we're going to have yummy desserts!"

"So . . . you read from the scrolls during a service, and then there's a big party with yummy desserts?

That's a Bat Mitzvah?" Zoey asked, wanting to make sure she had it straight.

"That's not all," Libby said. "I also do a mitzvah project, which means doing something to make the world a better place by helping others."

"What's your project?" Kate asked.

"Well, since I started volunteering at the food pantry, I've noticed they only give out canned and packaged goods, which must get really boring and isn't as healthy as having fresh produce," Libby said. "So I've started a vegetable patch to grow fresh produce to donate there. Dad helped me."

"That sounds like even more hard work," Priti groaned. "Are you going to have time for any *fun*?"

Libby laughed. "Gardening *is* fun. Come over and help me weed sometime! Maybe next Sunday?"

Priti looked skeptical. "Sounds like a great time . . . ," she said, "but I think I'm busy that day. Or any day when getting dirt under my fingernails is involved!"

"Do you get lots of presents?" Kate asked. "The kid whose Bar Mitzvah I went to did."

"Well, yes," Libby said.

"Who are you inviting?" Zoey asked.

"About a zillion relatives, half of whose names I don't even remember; kids from school—Josie, Gabe, Miles; Tyler, since I got to know him at the food pantry; a bunch of my friends from Hebrew school; and . . . Emily."

Zoey couldn't believe her ears.

"Emily Gooding?" Priti exclaimed. "Why are you inviting *her*?"

"*I* didn't invite her," Libby protested. "My mom did. My parents are friends with her parents, so Mom said I had to."

"Awkward," Kate said.

"I know." Libby sighed. "Trust me, I'm not happy about it."

Zoey wasn't happy about it either. Emily had taken over from Ivy Wallace as the head mean girl.

"We'll be having so much fun, we won't even notice she's there," Kate said.

"I hope so," Libby said. She turned to Zoey. "Zoey, I was wondering . . . Instead of getting me a present, could you design and make my dress for the party? I've got an idea of what I want, but if you made it, it would be really unique. I wouldn't have to worry that anyone else would be wearing the same dress."

"I'd love to!" Zoey said. "What do you have in mind?"

"I'd like a strapless dress with a sweetheart neckline, to go with the theme," Libby said. "But other than that, I'm happy to leave it up to your Sew Zoey genius."

"Oh, that sounds adorable!" Priti exclaimed. "Zoey . . . I know it's not my Bat Mitzvah . . . but can you make me a dress too? I want to look fab for Libby's big day!"

"While you're at it . . . ," Kate added.

"Okay, I'll make everyone dresses," Zoey said. "That way we'll all look extra special for the Bar Mitzvah."

"*Bat* Mitzvah," Libby corrected. "It's Bar Mitzvah for a boy and Bat Mitzvah for a girl."

"I hope I finally get this stuff right by the time your *Bat* Mitzvah happens!" Zoey groaned.

"You'll be fine," Libby reassured her. "Wait! I know . . . Let's go watch *Fiddler on the Roof*! My parents have it on Blu-ray. Then I'll teach you how to dance the hora."

"Is that the sideways dance?" Kate asked.

Libby laughed. "I *guess* you could call it that."

She gave them a quick lesson in the hora's footwork.

"Oh! It's kind of like doing the grapevine, but in a circle," Zoey said.

By the time Mrs. Flynn told them to go to bed, the girls were tired from so much giggling and doing the hora around the living room, and Zoey felt much more prepared for Libby's Bat Mitzvah.

CHAPTER 2

Twists on Tradition

I'm so excited to be going to my first Bat Mitzvah—and honored Libby asked me to design her dress for the big day. She had an idea of what she wanted, but I covered it in sweet, frilly flowers to make it go with her Bat Mitzvah theme of Sweet.

I'd much rather make the dress than have to get up and read all that stuff in a language that doesn't even have the same alphabet as English! Libby is working so hard to learn it all. But I think it's really cool she's carrying on a tradition, especially because it means so much to her grandfather.

I guess in a way I'm carrying on a family tradition too with Sew Zoey—my mom used to make and design her own clothes. It's nice to feel in touch with the past, but it's also fun to put your own modern twist on things.

"So have you had any thoughts about your dress?" Zoey asked Kate on the bus Monday morning.

"You know me," Kate said. "As long as it's simple and comfortable, I'll be happy. You're a lot better than I am with fashion ideas."

"You're right about the comfortable part—especially if we're going to be doing all that sideways dancing. . . . What's it called again?"

"The hora," Kate said. "But that's not the only kind of dancing they do at Bat Mitzvahs!"

"Wait, I have to learn *more* dances?" Zoey wailed, panicked.

"Don't worry," Kate said, giggling. "Nothing you haven't already seen at a school dance."

"Oh, good!" Zoey said. "I'm already afraid I'll say or do the wrong thing."

"You'll be fine," Kate reassured her. "It's going to be fun!"

Ms. Austen greeted them as they got off the bus, stylish as always in a navy suit and skirt with white piping.

"How was your weekend?" she asked with a smile.

"Great," Kate said.

"Fun!" Zoey agreed. "I love your suit."

"Thank you," Ms. Austen said. "I picked it up at a vintage consignment store last month. All it needed was a little tailoring and voilà!"

"It looks brand new," Kate said.

"Good pieces never go out of style, right, Zoey?" Ms. Austen said, giving Zoey a wink, and walked off to greet more students.

"Hey, Zo! Kate! What's up?" Priti had arrived,

full of more energy than anyone had a right to have first thing in the morning. "*Guess what!* I had the most fab idea for my dress for Libby's party."

"Let me guess," Kate said. "Sequins or something glittery are involved."

"Yes!" Priti exclaimed. "How did you know?"

Zoey and Kate exchanged glances. Lately, Priti had been wearing Goth-style clothing—dressing all in black or in other dark colors—but she still loved anything sparkly. Luckily, black was the perfect color to wear to a party.

"What else do you have in mind?" Zoey asked. "What's more fab than sequins?"

"Purple!" Priti declared. "I'd like a long-sleeved sheath dress in purple sequins. Kind of like this one."

She showed Zoey a picture of a dress she'd printed from the *Très Chic* website.

"I can make something like that—no problem!" Zoey assured her.

"That's so pretty," Kate said. "It's simple, but the sequins make it sparkly."

"I'm calling it . . . Effervescent Grape Diva Style."

The girls were laughing at Priti's humor when Ivy, Zoey's longtime nemesis, walked by with Emily, who was fast becoming the new queen bee of Mapleton Prep.

"I'm so glad it's tacos and salad for lunch today," Emily said. "It's about the only halfway edible thing the cafeteria serves."

"Oh . . . yeah. Actually, I brought lunch from home today," Ivy replied.

Zoey watched as Emily stopped and stared at Ivy.

"Why would you do that?" she asked. "Just throw it away and buy the tacos!"

Ivy laughed, but her face flushed from the neck up. "Oh, sure. Right."

As they walked into school, Zoey saw Ivy reach into her backpack, pull out a brown lunch bag, and throw it into the nearest garbage can.

"Can you believe that?" Kate exclaimed. "The people who come to the food pantry would love a homemade lunch, and Ivy just threw hers in the garbage because of Emily!"

"I know." Zoey sighed, following Ivy and Emily into the building. "What a waste of food."

Libby's Bat Mitzvah project at the food pantry had already opened Zoey's eyes to the issue of hunger in their town. Zoey was determined to find a way to help Libby in any way she could.

Soon it was time for their new electives. The woodshop smelled of pine and linseed oils and was stocked with saws of all kinds. While she had been excited to start, seeing the sharp teeth of the saws gave Zoey second thoughts.

"What if I cut off one of my fingers and can't finish Libby's Bat Mitzvah dress?" she asked Priti.

"Zo, if you cut off a finger, finishing Libby's dress is going to be the least of your problems!" Priti observed.

"If the safety procedures are followed, everyone should leave this classroom with all ten digits," Mr. Weldon, the industrial arts teacher, assured them. "Your well-being is the number-one priority in this shop."

"See!" Priti said. "Don't worry. You'll be able to make Libby's dress—and my dress, too!"

Mr. Weldon spent the first half of the period

going through a handout on safety rules.

"There will be a quiz on the safety rules on Friday, so please pay attention. Rule number one: *ALWAYS* wear eye protection. If I see anyone using equipment without goggles, it's an automatic detention," he said. "Rule number two: Avoid wearing long sleeves or loose clothing to class since it can get caught in the machines." He pointed to his ponytail. "And rule number three: See my long hippie hair? It must be tied back during class, and so should yours."

"But I don't want to get a kink in my hair," Emily complained. She had long, straight, reddish brown hair and was very proud of it.

"Personally, I'd be less concerned about that and a little more worried about the possibility of accidentally getting my hair—and the face attached to it—pulled into a saw," Mr. Weldon said. He walked over and handed Emily a hair tie from his stash. "Here you go," he said, and Emily reluctantly used it to pull back her hair. "Now, for the grand tour."

Zoey listened and watched as Mr. Weldon walked them around the shop, giving them an overview of the equipment.

"This is the worst elective ever," Emily whispered as Mr. Weldon explained the uses of a band saw. "I can't wait till it's over."

"At least we have Fashion Fun Club to look forward to after school," Ivy whispered back.

Zoey wished they'd be quiet because she wanted to make sure she didn't miss any safety instructions.

"And things with the club are so much better organized now that Zoey isn't the treasurer anymore," Emily whispered, but it was obvious she wanted Zoey to hear.

Priti gave Zoey a sympathetic glance.

"Ladies, if you have expertise about the band saw, please share it with all of us," Mr. Weldon said, looking straight at Ivy and Emily. "Otherwise, I'd appreciate your full attention."

Each saw was scarier than the next as far as Zoey was concerned. The radial arm saw, the miter saw, the table saw—and then they got to the other equipment: sanders, planers, and jointers.

"That was the scariest elective ever," she told Priti after the bell rang.

"But you manage to work a sewing machine just

fine without being scared," Priti said. "Just think of the saw as, you know, like a really big sewing machine."

"I guess," Zoey said, as she gathered her books to head to her next class. "One with really *big teeth*."

Emily and Ivy were just ahead of Priti and Zoey as they filed out of the classroom.

"I thought you were going to get a skirt like mine and wear it today," Emily told Ivy.

"I was . . . ," Ivy said. "I mean, I am. I just . . . haven't been able to get to the mall to get it. My mom's been too busy to drive me."

"We could go on Wednesday after school," Emily said. "My mom could drive. I want to get some of those new woven bracelets I saw in *Seventeen*. They're so cute."

"I can't," Ivy said. "I'm busy. I have a . . . dentist appointment."

"Didn't you go to the dentist last week?" Emily said.

"Oh . . . yeah. But . . . I have a cavity," Ivy mumbled. "So I have to get it filled."

"Does it sound to you like Ivy's making excuses?"

Priti quietly commented to Zoey, stopping so Emily and Ivy could walk farther ahead of them down the noisy hallway.

"I don't know," Zoey said, watching as her frequent frenemy turned the corner. "But Ivy definitely seems a little . . . different lately."

"Hey, Zoey! Priti! Wait up!"

Gabe Monaco, Zoey's friend, then crush, now friend again, caught up with them, breathless.

"Am I glad I found you! I just had my first home economics class," he panted.

"Oh, yeah, we just had industrial arts," Priti said. "Zoey's freaked out by all the saws."

"Who knew there were so many different kinds?" Zoey retorted. "And all of them are *very* sharp."

"Well, I seem to be all thumbs with a sewing machine," Gabe quipped. "I can't tell a bobbin and a spindle apart. And we have to make an apron for the class competition before we can get to the fun stuff like baking. So . . . Zoey, I was wondering if I could ask you for help."

"Sure!" Zoey said. "It's really not that hard, I promise."

Gabe looked at her skeptically.

"You know how you feel about a band saw?" he asked. "That's me with a sewing machine. I can just see me sewing my finger into a seam . . . if I could ever get the machine to work."

"That's better than accidentally cutting off half your thumb," Zoey argued.

"Eww! Can you stop with the gross-out competition?" Priti said. "I'm going to throw up!"

Gabe and Zoey laughed.

"Okay, competition over," Gabe said. "Catch you guys later . . . and thanks, Zoey!"

"Dad, can you drive me to Libby's house on Sunday around lunchtime?" Zoey asked her father at dinner on Thursday night. "I want her to finalize her Bat Mitzvah dress design so I can start work. I've got four dresses to make before her big day!"

Zoey wasn't sure if it was her imagination, or if it was the lighting in the kitchen, but it looked like her dad was starting to . . . blush?

"I . . . Marcus, can you drive Zoey on Sunday?"

"I think so—I'll text Allie after dinner to make

sure we don't have anything planned." Marcus eyed his father with a raised eyebrow. "Why, Dad? Do you have a date or something?"

It definitely wasn't her imagination, Zoey thought. Her dad *was* blushing!

"As a matter of fact, yes, I do have a date," he admitted. "We're going to a museum."

"You and the Mystery Lady?" Zoey asked.

Dad nodded.

"Very cultured," Marcus said, grinning. "So are we ever going to meet the Mystery Lady?"

"Oh, you'll meet her," Dad said.

"When?" Zoey asked.

"Uh . . . soon," Dad replied.

Zoey noticed he changed the subject to football as quickly as he could! Usually, Dad was pretty open about his dates. She wondered what made this one different.

"So how long do you think it'll be before Dad actually introduces us to the Mystery Girlfriend?" Marcus asked Zoey as he was driving her to Libby's house on Sunday.

"It feels like it'll never happen." Zoey sighed. "But I hope it's soon, because I'm really curious."

"Me too," Marcus said. "It's hilarious how he blushes and gets all shy whenever we talk about her."

"Do you think that means it's . . . serious? Like getting-married-again serious?"

"I think you should at least let him introduce her to us before you start marrying them off, Zo," Marcus said. "You worry too much."

Dad getting remarried to the Mystery Girlfriend wasn't the only thing worrying Zoey, though.

"Is everything okay with you and Allie?" she asked.

"Yeah," Marcus said. He sounded surprised. "Why do you ask?"

"It's just that you seem to be around a lot more than you usually are," Zoey observed. "And she's been around a lot less."

Marcus focused on the road ahead and didn't say anything right away.

"I mean, it's true, she's been really busy lately. Like, whenever I want to hang out, she's got something to do." He pulled the car into Libby's driveway and then turned to face Zoey. "But that's because she really *is* busy with all her blog stuff, not because there's anything wrong."

"Okay," Zoey said. "I was just wondering, that's all."

She grabbed her sketchbook. "I'm glad you weren't busy. It gave us a chance to hang out."

"I love it!" Libby exclaimed when Zoey showed her the sketch for her Bat Mitzvah dress. "It's even better than I imagined!"

"Do you know what kind of fabric you want?" Zoey asked. "If not, we could go to A Stitch in Time and look at material."

"You choose," Libby said. "Between volunteering at the food pantry and Hebrew tutoring and Hebrew school, I'm already crazy busy. Plus, I have to do the work for my mitzvah project. Today I have to weed the vegetable patch, otherwise the produce won't grow well."

"I can help you with that," Zoey offered.

"Really? You'll help?" Libby looked so relieved.

"Sure. It's a nice day; we'll be outside. How hard can it be?"

A lot harder than she thought, Zoey realized after they'd been doing it for a while. She had crescents of dirt caked beneath her fingernails, and her back and knees hurt from kneeling and bending over to pull weeds! Libby's little sister, Sophie, came out and "helped" too, although Libby got upset when she pulled up an onion instead of the weeds and it had to be replanted.

But when they were done, the rows among the pumpkins, squashes, onions, broccoli, and cabbages that Libby was growing for the food pantry looked much better.

"These aren't my favorite vegetables, but they're all that I could grow now. I checked with the people at the garden center," Libby explained. "I'll be able to grow a bigger variety of things in the spring and summer."

"Look at the size of this pumpkin! It's enormous!" Zoey exclaimed.

"That's my prize specimen," Libby said.

"We call him the Pumpkinator," Sophie cheerfully chimed in.

"It's so great that you're doing this," Zoey said. "It's a lot of work to grow all these vegetables."

"I know," Libby said. "But volunteering at the food pantry made me realize how lucky we are. I mean, I've always just taken it for granted that Mom makes us great meals all the time—and not only that, we get to go out to restaurants and get takeout sometimes when Mom's too tired to cook. The families that come in to the food pantry don't seem so different from mine."

"That's true," Zoey said. "Volunteering at the pet shelter made me realize how lucky Buttons is to live with Aunt Lulu and Uncle John and not be abandoned on the street to fend for herself."

"Now, that's something I really can't imagine," Libby said. "Buttons, a street dog having to forage for food herself. She'd miss her treats too much!"

Zoey laughed. "I know. She's turning into a fluffy treat-a-holic."

Libby stood up and surveyed the vegetable patch. Her cheeks and the tip of her nose were tinged pink from both the chill in the air and the exertion of pulling weeds.

"That looks so much better," she said. "I don't know about you guys, but my fingers and toes are starting to get numb. Let's get some hot chocolate."

"Yum!" Zoey exclaimed.

"Me too! Me too!" Sophie jumped around in excitement as they walked toward the house.

As soon as they opened the back door, Mrs. Flynn called out from the kitchen, "Take off your shoes and wash your hands!"

Libby turned to Zoey as they were scrubbing the dirt from under their fingernails. "When we're done washing up, can we get your sketch pad? I can't wait to show the dress to Mom!"

"Sure!" Zoey said.

When they went into the kitchen, they made big steaming mugs of hot chocolate, with mini marshmallows floating on top, for themselves and Sophie. Zoey wrapped her cold fingers around the mug to warm her hands.

"Look at the dress Zoey designed for my Bat Mitzvah party," Libby told her mom, proudly holding open Zoey's sketchbook. "Isn't it perfect?"

Mrs. Flynn looked at the sketch. She didn't smile. She didn't say anything. Zoey's heart sank. *She doesn't like it,* she thought.

"It's a delightful dress, Zoey," Mrs. Flynn said. "You're very talented." Zoey waited for the "but," and sure enough, it came. "But I just don't think a strapless dress is appropriate for a twelve-year-old girl, especially for a religious event."

"I think it's pretty!" Sophie said.

"But, *Mooooom,*" Libby groaned. "It's *sooooo* gorgeous and I've been to other Bat Mitzvahs where girls wore dresses just like it! Well, not *just* like it, because it's totally unique, but you know what I mean."

"I understand, sweetheart, but those other girls aren't my daughter," Mrs. Flynn pointed out. "You are."

Libby wasn't looking very happy about that fact at that particular moment, even though she and her mom usually got along really well.

"That's *so unfair*, Mom!" she said. "You said having a Bat Mitzvah means I'm becoming an adult in the Jewish community, so why can't I choose what I want to wear?"

"Because I'm still you're mother," Mrs. Flynn said, "and I'm telling you that it's inappropriate."

As the argument became more and more heated, Zoey tried to shrink into the background. She felt awkward—and awful. The last thing she wanted to do was to cause trouble between Libby and her mom.

By the time Mrs. Flynn left the kitchen, telling Sophie to come upstairs to do her reading for school, Libby was steaming more than the hot chocolate.

"I can't believe her!" she said. "Why can't I wear what I want to wear? It's supposed to be *my* day!"

"I could . . . make some . . . modifications," Zoey ventured. She felt caught in the middle, wanting to make everyone happy but without any idea of how, exactly, to go about doing it.

"No, don't do it yet," Libby said. "I have a plan."

"What's that?" Zoey asked, curious.

"I'm going to call Aunt Lexie," Libby said. "She knows fashion, and she's way cooler than Mom.

Maybe she'll be able to convince her that a strapless dress is okay."

If anyone could convince Libby's mom, Lexie could.

"Good idea," Zoey said. "I really hope it works!"

CHAPTER 3

Balancing Act

Fashion is about balancing shape and volume—like when you wear a flowing top with lots of interest and slim line pants, or a tight, solid-colored top and a patterned skirt. It's so much easier to find balance with fabrics than it is with people. Like . . . what do you do when you want to make one person happy, but you end up making another person unhappy? Life would be so much easier if you could just make everyone happy all the time, wouldn't it? I just want to be like Lady Justice, always doing the right thing, even when blindfolded. Even without a blindfold, it's not that easy.

When I explained Libby's dress situation to Dad, he said, "Welcome to my world!" He said he often has to make hard decisions that he knows will make either Marcus or me—or even sometimes both of us—unhappy, but that's being a parent. I guess there isn't always a 100 percent "right" solution to every problem.

Later that afternoon, after his date at the museum, Dad came to pick up Zoey from Libby's.

"How was your day of art appreciation with you know who?" Zoey asked when she got into the car.

"Very nice," Dad said, smiling. "I know *way* more about art than I did this morning!"

"So . . . are you going to be going to museums a lot now?" Zoey asked.

"I don't know about that," Dad said. "I've seen

enough paintings for a month or two at least. Sports are definitely more my thing."

Zoey thought about asking him when they'd meet his date, but then he started telling her all about the paintings he'd seen, and she lost the courage to do it.

A car was in the driveway when they pulled up at home.

"Oh, Allie's here!" Zoey said.

"She hasn't been around so much recently," Dad said.

"Marcus says she's been really busy with her blog and stuff," Zoey said quickly. "It's not because there's anything wrong."

"I wasn't saying there was," Dad said. "Just making the observation."

But when they came into the house, it seemed like maybe there was something wrong, because it sounded like Marcus and Allie were fighting downstairs in the basement. Even though the door was closed, and Zoey and Dad couldn't hear what they were saying, it was clear from the volume and the tone that they weren't very happy with each other.

"Looks like there might be trouble in paradise." Dad sighed. "I'm going to go turn on the football game and let them have their privacy."

Zoey wanted to stay in the kitchen, so she could try to hear what was going on, but Dad gestured with his thumb that she should scram too. Giving Dad a worried look, she headed upstairs to her room to work on the designs for Priti's and Kate's dresses.

The sketch for Priti's dress was coming along when Zoey heard the front door shut more loudly than usual, followed by the sound of Allie—who had just gotten her driver's license—starting her car and pulling out of the driveway. A minute later, Marcus came crashing up the stairs and slammed the door to his bedroom.

Zoey wondered if she should leave him alone to let him calm down, but she decided against it, since she wanted to help. She walked down the hall and tapped on his door.

"What?"

"It's Zoey. Can I come in?"

"Yeah, I guess."

Her brother was sprawled on his bed, with his arm over his face.

"Are you okay?" Zoey asked.

"I'm fine," Marcus mumbled, his face still covered by his arm.

"You don't seem that okay," Zoey said. "Are you sure everything is all right? It sounded like you and Allie were fighting."

"You think?" Marcus said.

"So . . . did you manage to work everything out?"

Marcus didn't say anything. Zoey watched his Adam's apple rise and fall as he took a deep breath and then swallowed.

"No." He lowered his arms, revealing eyes that were red and damp. "She . . . broke up with me."

"Oh no!" Zoey exclaimed. She sat down on the bed next to her brother and gave his leg a comforting squeeze.

"I didn't even see it coming," Marcus said. "I mean, she'd been busy a lot . . . and we'd been arguing more than usual, but . . . I didn't think she'd *end* it."

"Did she say why?" Zoey asked.

"Something about it getting too serious. She said she's not ready for serious," Marcus said. "I told her I would take things more slowly, but that didn't make a difference. She just wanted to end it, and that was that."

He put his arm back over his face, and his chest heaved.

"I'm sorry, Marcus," she said. "I know you really like her."

"Yeah. Whatever."

Her brother rolled over, turned on his music, and kept his back to Zoey. He obviously needed time to himself.

As she walked back to her room, she wondered how Allie's decision was going to affect their friendship. She'd been friends with Allie before Marcus started dating her. But he was her brother—and it was clear he was hurting. Badly.

It feels like I'm getting stuck in the middle of everything right now, Zoey thought with a sigh as she picked up her pencil and went back to work on the sketches for Priti's and Kate's dresses.

"So how's your Bat Mitzvah project going?" Priti asked Libby at lunch on Tuesday.

"Good!" Libby said. "Zoey helped me weed on Sunday."

"That was hard work!" Zoey said.

"But now I've got a new plan," Libby said.

"Is that why you were in such deep conversation with the head of the food pantry when we were volunteering yesterday?" Kate asked.

Libby nodded. "He said that in order to be able to safely accommodate all the produce I plan to grow and raise money to buy, they'll need a new industrial fridge, because the one they have isn't big enough."

"Uh-oh. That sounds expensive," Priti said.

"It is." Libby sighed. "Two-thousand-dollar expensive."

Zoey whistled. "That's a *lot* of money."

"I know," Libby admitted. "But the food pantry director said we might be able to get a discount because it's a nonprofit. I'm determined to make this happen no matter what it takes."

"This might sound like a stupid question but . . . how?" Kate asked. "You'd have to babysit every weekend for . . . *years* . . . to make that much money."

"Well, a lot of people give money as a Bat Mitzvah gift, and I talked to my parents about using part of that toward the fridge," Libby explained. "But since I'm not sure that will be enough, I figured I'd have a bake sale—after all, the theme of my party is Sweet, right?"

"But even a bake sale might not raise enough," Zoey said.

"I know," Libby said. "But I want to try."

"We can help," Zoey said, remembering how Ivy just threw away a perfectly good packed lunch.

"I can make stuff to sell at the bake sale!" Priti offered. She and her mom were well-known for their baking. The Holbrookes saved the day on the dessert front at Aunt Lulu and Uncle John's surprise wedding, when the bakery making the wedding cupcakes flooded.

"Me too," Zoey said. "I'd rather bake than weed the vegetable patch!"

"I can make sugar cookies with vegetable decorations," Kate said. "Oh wait, but then people might think they taste like carrots and broccoli."

"Eww! Broccoli cookies!" Priti grimaced. "No, thanks."

"Maybe skip the veggie decorations," Libby said with a grin. "But thanks, you guys, for offering to bake. I'm going to need all the help I can get!"

After school, Zoey was in her room working on the dress designs for her friends. She still didn't know what to do about Libby's Bat Mitzvah dress. Libby's mom was unhappy with the design as it was, and Libby didn't want Zoey to change a single thing. Meanwhile, she really wanted to call Allie to see if they could remain friends, but she was afraid that if Marcus found out, he might feel betrayed and be angry with Zoey. And Marcus seemed upset enough at the moment without her adding to his problems.

She sighed, putting down her pencil and gazing at the sketches. At least Kate's and Priti's dresses were looking pretty great. Now it was time to start playing with ideas for her own outfit.

"Hey, Zo?"

Marcus was standing in the doorway, his hair sticking up in all directions like he'd been running his hand through it. He'd been moping around in front of the TV and eating chocolate chips when she got home from school, and he'd barely even grunted hello when she came in, which wasn't really like him.

"What's up?" Zoey asked.

Her brother sat down on the edge of her bed and started fidgeting with the piping on one of her throw pillows.

"I was just wondering. . . . You know how you're friends with Allie?"

"Well, yeah," Zoey said. "Except I'm not sure I am, exactly, now that the two of you have broken up. It's kind of awkward."

"I thought maybe . . . you could get together with her and find out, you know, what's really going on."

Zoey stared at her brother. "Wait . . . you want me to spy on Allie?"

"No!" Marcus exclaimed. "Not spy on her, exactly. Just . . . get the real scoop on why she broke up with me."

"But you said you were fighting and she was busy a lot."

"I know, but . . . we got along so well."

"Except for the fighting part," Zoey pointed out.

"But that was only recently," Marcus said. "Please, will you do it?"

"I don't know. It seems kind of weird. Allie's my friend, remember? She was my friend before you started going out with her."

"I know," Marcus said. "And I feel bad asking you to do this. But . . . I really need to know what happened. It just seems so out of the blue, her just wanting to end it like this."

"Okay, I'll do it." Zoey sighed. "I'll call and see about getting together."

"Thanks, Zo," Marcus said. "But promise me you won't let on that I'm upset we broke up. I don't want her to feel sorry for me or anything."

"Your secret is safe with me," Zoey said.

"Cool. You're the best."

"I know," Zoey said jokingly.

When he left the room, she stared at Allie's name on her cell phone, willing herself to dial. Was it going to be awkward to speak to her?

Here goes nothing, she thought, pressing the call button.

Allie sounded happy to hear from Zoey.

"Hi! Zoey! I . . . wasn't sure if I'd hear from you, what with me and Marcus breaking up and everything."

"Did you want to?" Zoey asked.

"Of course!" Allie said. "You're my friend, aren't you?"

"I think so," Zoey said. "I mean, I hope so."

"Do you want to get together tomorrow?" Allie asked. "We could go get ice cream after school."

"Sure!" Zoey said, relieved she didn't have to suggest it. She really wanted to stay friends with Allie, but being a spy for Marcus didn't feel like the best way to do it. She hated seeing her brother so sad, though, and she wanted to help him, somehow.

"Great. I'll pick you up after school. See you tomorrow!"

"Yeah. See you!"

It was a relief to hang up, pick up her pencil, and get back to noodling around with dress ideas for her to wear to Libby's Bat Mitzvah. At least that didn't fill her with a confusing mix of emotions!

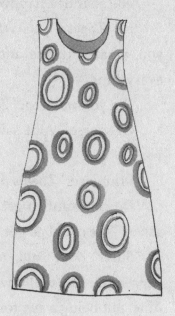

CHAPTER 4

Bat Mitzvah Belles

I've designed these dresses for my friends to wear to Libby's Bat Mitzvah—sparkly for Priti and simple clean lines for Kate. I need to start getting on with my own outfit; otherwise, I'm not going to have time to make anything. There's just been so much other stuff going on. Complicated stuff, too. Sometimes it feels like life is a knitting bag, where all the wool has gotten totally tangled up, and I wish I could just get it all rolled into neat balls again.

Zoey picked nervously at a loose thread on her backpack as she stood in front of Mapleton Prep, waiting for Allie to pick her up. She'd never felt the slightest bit funny about hanging out with Allie before, but things were different now. Marcus expected Zoey to make this into a fact-finding spy mission instead of just a chilling-out and chatting session.

Allie honked the horn and waved when she pulled her car up at the curb, seeming just like the friend she'd been before she and Marcus started dating.

Maybe it won't be so awkward after all, Zoey thought as she waved back, ran over, opened the door, and climbed into the passenger seat.

Allie leaned over to give her a hug. "Zoey! I'm so glad we could get together! I'm really sorry about . . .

you know, the breakup. It was a hard decision, and I was afraid you wouldn't want to be friends with me anymore. That would make everything twice as bad."

So why did you break up with him in the first place? Zoey wondered.

Allie started the car and drove away from the school. "Is Poppa's Pastry Shop okay?"

"Sounds good to me," Zoey said. "Their hot chocolate is the best."

On the way to the café, they compared notes on their respective blogs and talked about fashion, just as they always had.

Well, not quite. . . . Zoey felt like Marcus was an unspoken presence in the backseat, urging her to find out what really happened between him and Allie.

It wasn't until they were sitting with their steaming mugs of hot cocoa that she finally summoned up the courage to ask.

"Allie . . . can I ask why you broke up with my brother? It seemed like you guys really got along. Well, at least to me."

Her friend stared down into her mug.

"We did get along. . . . I mean, we do get along . . . and I really like Marcus, Zo, he's a great guy. . . . It's just . . ."

Allie picked up her spoon and started poking at the rapidly melting whipped cream atop the hot chocolate.

"It's just what?" Zoey insisted.

"It's just that he was getting too serious. You know, that he liked me a lot more than I was ready for. We're young, Zoey. We're not even out of high school. Who knows what's going to happen, right?"

"I guess," Zoey said. "But wasn't he willing to slow things down?"

"He said that, but he gave me a ring. I mean, I know it wasn't an *engagement* ring or anything, but it still looked really expensive, and I felt guilty taking it from him. It felt too . . . serious," Allie explained. "And I'm not ready for serious. I'm too young to be tied down forever."

Zoey was just thinking she could see Allie's point of view—and feeling a little conflicted for doing so—when her friend's phone vibrated loudly against the table. Allie picked it up and held it under the table to read a text message. She smiled, and her cheeks were tinged pink.

"Can you understand that, Zo?" Allie said. "I really hope that you and I can stay friends." Even though Allie was talking to her, her eyes kept glancing downward, and Zoey could tell she was typing into her phone.

"How is Marcus doing?" Allie asked. "I really didn't want to hurt him, you know. He's such a great guy."

He is *a great guy*, Zoey thought. Except now, thanks to him, Zoey was in another awkward situation. She'd promised her brother that she wouldn't tell Allie that he was miserable, but if she told her friend anything else, she'd be lying.

"He's fine," Zoey finally said, feeling horrible about being dishonest. She had to think of a plausible activity that Marcus could be keeping himself busy with, instead of saying what he was actually doing, which was moping around the house looking sad. "He's been . . . practicing a lot with his band."

"That's cool," Allie said, although she was looking down in her lap again, her thumbs clearly busy with her phone. "How are the mad guitar skills going?"

"Oh, he's getting much better!" Zoey said. "Yeah, he's really coming along. You'll be wishing you were still going out when he sells out an arena."

Allie laughed, but Zoey wasn't sure if it was at what she'd said or if it was something Allie'd read on her phone, because that's where Allie's eyes were focused. "Yeah, I'm sure I will," she said.

It was strange and confusing to Zoey that Allie seemed more interested in her phone than in the face-to-face conversation they were supposedly having. She'd never been that way before when they hung out. Did Allie think she was boring all of a sudden?

It was almost a relief when Allie dropped Zoey off at home. She pulled the car into the driveway, but she didn't come in like she usually would.

"Say hi to Marcus and your dad for me," Allie said as Zoey got out of the car.

Zoey didn't say she would. She just said, "Bye— good seeing you," and then headed for the house.

She'd barely gotten both feet through the door-way when Marcus pounced.

"What happened?" he asked. "What did she say?"

"Can I at least put down my backpack?" Zoey complained. "Sheesh!"

Marcus followed her into the kitchen and watched as Zoey put down her backpack, took off her jacket and hung it up, and got a glass of water.

"So?" he said. "How was it?"

"It was fine," Zoey said. "It was a normal get-together. We talked about all the same kinds of stuff we used to talk about before you two started dating, and then I asked her why she broke up with you, and she told me the same thing she told you—that she wasn't ready to be serious."

"I said I was okay with slowing down," Marcus complained. "But she broke up with me anyway."

"The ring freaked her out," Zoey told him. "A lot. I think that was what did it."

"I don't understand girls," Marcus said. "You try and do something nice, like buy them a present, and it freaks them out and makes them break up with you. Go figure!"

He turned to head down the basement stairs. Zoey could tell it was going to be a loud night as Marcus began to take out his angst over Allie on the drums.

The next day at lunch, Zoey told her friends about her afternoon with Allie.

"I get that she doesn't want to be tied down. I mean, they are still in high school," she said. "But . . . I don't know."

"What?" Kate asked. "It seems like a normal reason to break up."

"Maybe it's hard to be objective because Marcus is your brother?" Libby said.

"Could be," Zoey said. "But . . . it wasn't just that. It was the way she kept texting the whole time we were talking. She kept her phone in her lap, like she was trying not to be obvious, but it was obvious, anyway. And she kept blushing."

Zoey twisted her napkin into a little ball. "I'm pretty sure I wasn't saying anything that would have made her blush. There was one time when her face turned red, and we were talking about the new bag she's selling on her blog. Not very blush-worthy if you ask me."

"That sounds pretty suspicious," Priti said. "I bet you anything she's seeing someone else, and *that's* why she broke up with Marcus. I think the whole 'ring present freaking her out' was just an excuse."

"You do?" Zoey said. "To tell you the truth, I was wondering about that too."

"But you don't know for sure," Libby said. "It's just a hunch."

"I know." Zoey sighed. "And I don't even want to think about it. I feel so bad—Allie's my friend and Marcus is my brother. I don't want either of them to be hurt. I wish they'd never started dating in the first place!"

"But they had a lot fun while they were together," Kate pointed out. "If they never dated in the first place, they would have missed out on that."

Zoey had to admit that was true. "Yeah, when Dad talks about Mom, he says, ''Tis better to have loved and lost than never to have loved at all.'"

"Maybe," Priti said. "But it's definitely better to have loved and not have been lied to."

"Do you think I should tell Marcus that I suspect Allie is dating someone else?" Zoey asked. "He's my brother, and I'd feel awful if he finds out it's true and that I thought she was but never warned him."

"But what if you're wrong?" argued Kate.

"That would be really unfair to Allie," Libby agreed. "And she's your friend. Or at least I think she is."

"Maybe you should just keep doing detective work," Priti suggested. "Not exactly spying, but . . . Well, just keeping an *eye* on things when you see Allie. In case you pick up any additional clues."

"Okay. Marcus does deserve to know the truth," Zoey said. "It's just . . . this whole situation is so awkward. It's no fun at all!"

"Moving on to happier subjects . . . I *love* the design you did for my dress!" Priti said. "It's perfect!"

"I love it, too," Libby agreed. "And Kate's is fab."

"I like the dress *you're* wearing today," Zoey said. "Florals really suit you."

"You were wearing something floral like that

when we volunteered at the food pantry the other night," Kate said. "But it was more like shorts."

"That was my floral romper," Libby said. "I'm kind of obsessed with floral stuff at the moment. I really like wearing it because it makes me feel feminine."

"Well, it looks good on you," Zoey said. "Maybe that's your signature look."

"Like wearing black combined with lots of bling is mine," Priti said with a dramatic arm wave that caught Zoey's carton of chocolate milk and tipped it toward the edge of the table—and straight for Kate's lap.

Luckily, Kate, with her athlete's reflexes, caught the carton before any of the liquid could land on her light tan corduroys.

"I'm glad chocolate milk didn't end up being my signature look!" she said.

"Nice save, Kate," Gabe said. "I'm impressed." Gabe had walked over from where he was sitting a few tables away.

Kate smiled and then put the carton on the table. "All in a day's work," she said.

"So . . . uh . . . Zoey," Gabe said, "you know I asked you about helping me with home ec?"

"Sure," Zoey said. "What's up?"

"I still have to make that apron, and I need your help."

"Sounds like it's time for that sewing lesson we talked about," Zoey said. "If you want to come over tomorrow, I can show you the ropes."

"You're the best!" Gabe said, looking relieved. "Tomorrow after school. Awesome."

As he walked back to his table, Priti shook her head. "Make sure you don't do it for him. Dad says he wished he learned how to sew, because now that my parents are divorced, he has to pay someone to sew his buttons back on when they fall off," she said. "Mom always used to do it for him."

"Maybe I should teach Dad and Marcus how to sew buttons," Zoey said. "Dad used to send his clothes out to be fixed, but ever since I've learned how to sew, I've been doing it."

"It goes both ways," Priti said. "Mom had to ask the neighbor how to use a drill when she wanted to hang a shelf in my room, because Dad had always done stuff like that. That's why I'm glad we're taking industrial arts."

Zoey wasn't so sure. She'd rather use a sewing machine than a drill any day!

------- CHAPTER 5 -------

Love Is a Battlefield . . . Or a Bicycle?

Two people who I really care about, and who were dating, broke up, and it's sad—not to mention it makes for some serious awkwardness.

Movies and fairy tales make love look so easy. But it sure doesn't seem all that easy in real life. I wonder why they don't say, "Hey, being in love looks like a lot of fun, but you know what? It's a lot harder than it looks!" Is it like riding a bicycle—the more you fall in love the easier it gets?

Luckily for me, I'm *waaaaay* too busy to fall in love— or even in *LIKE*—with anyone. I'm also too busy to go on a bike ride. I've got four special dresses to make for my friend's Bat Mitzvah!

"Have you already started making my dress for Libby's Bat Mitzvah?" Kate asked when Zoey got on the bus the next morning.

"No, not yet," Zoey said. "I made Priti's first. But I was planning on starting yours tonight."

"It's just . . . I'm having second thoughts about the circle pattern on the dress," Kate said. "I was wondering if maybe we could go with something a bit more . . . floral."

"Really?" Zoey said, gaping at her friend in disbelief. "Floral? For you? Are you sure?"

"I think so," Kate said. "Why? What's the matter with floral?"

"Nothing," Zoey replied. "It just doesn't seem like you at all. What made you change your mind?"

Kate's face flushed. "Nothing," she mumbled, shrugging her shoulders. "I just wanted a change of pace, that's all."

Zoey had a feeling there was more to Kate's request than she was letting on, but since Kate obviously didn't want to talk about whatever it was, she just said, "No problem. I'll see what I can come up with."

"Thanks," Kate said. "You're the best, Zo!"

"I've got great news," Libby told her friends at lunch. "I've gotten permission to hold my bake sale to benefit the food pantry at the high school football game next weekend!"

"Wow! That's so awesome," Zoey said. "Those games are always pretty crowded."

"Oh yeah. You're going to raise a fortune," Priti agreed.

"There's just one catch," Libby said. "In order to make lots of money, I need lots of things to sell. Are you guys still willing to help me bake?"

"Of course!" Kate said. "I'll make my mom's famous turtle brownie bars. They always sell out whenever we have fund-raisers for the swim team and the soccer team."

"I can make red velvet cupcakes," Priti offered. "And snickerdoodles. I love snickerdoodles! Also, I like just saying the name. Snickerdoodles!"

Zoey giggled at her friend, who kept whispering "snickerdoodles" under her breath.

"I'll make brownies," Zoey said. "And I can make some chocolate chip cookies if Marcus hasn't eaten all the chocolate chips."

"Oh . . . breakup chocolate?" Priti asked.

Zoey nodded.

"Anything chocolatey sells fast," Kate said.

"Thank you! You guys are the best," Libby exclaimed. "With your help, I'm going to raise the money for the food pantry fridge in no time!"

Gabe took the bus home with Zoey after school. After they'd had a quick snack in the kitchen, Zoey said, "Come on, my sewing machine is in the dining room. Time to make your apron!"

Gabe groaned as he got up and took the material and basic pattern for his apron out of his backpack.

"I'm so not looking forward to this. Can't we just make the brownies for Libby's bake sale?"

"We can, but then you'll flunk home ec. Come on—I'll show you want to do," Zoey said. "It's not that hard. Really—I promise."

They spread the material on the table, and Zoey showed Gabe how to pin the pieces of the apron pattern to the fabric. She started cutting the cloth, then held out the shears.

"Okay, your turn."

Gabe looked at the scissors with dismay.

"What . . . You want *me* to cut it? But . . . what happens if I make a mistake?"

Zoey laughed. "It won't be the first time a mistake has happened at this table. Besides, I've double-checked everything. Like Jan, the lady who owns A Stitch in Time, says, 'Measure twice, cut once.'"

Gabe kept his hands firmly by his side.

"Just do it!" Zoey urged.

Gabe took the scissors with just about the same

reluctance he would've had if Zoey were handing him a dirty diaper.

"Well . . . here goes nothing."

Zoey watched as he cut the fabric with all the confidence of a nursery school kid learning how to cut craft paper.

"It's okay, Gabe. It's not the end of the world if you make a mistake."

"Easy for you to say, Miss Fashion Designer Extraordinaire," Gabe said, his eyes not leaving the fabric. "But I won't pass home ec if I don't produce this stupid apron."

"If you make a mistake, we'll figure out how to cover it up or make it seem like it was on purpose," Zoey assured him. "Sometimes mistakes turn into something great."

Slowly and carefully, Gabe cut out the pieces for the apron.

"Good job!" Zoey said. "See, that wasn't so bad."

"Yes, it was," Gabe said. "I think I'm getting a cramp in my hand."

Zoey laughed again. "Ouch. That means you need to loosen your death grip on the scissors!" she said. "Now to sew the seams on each of the pieces so the edges are nicely finished and then . . . put them all together."

"You make it sound so easy." Gabe sighed.

"It is easy," Zoey said. "Come on, I'll show you how to do seams."

She ran a seam on a scrap of fabric.

"See, you just have to keep the fabric straight and make sure it doesn't get bunched up," she said. "Go ahead and try it."

"Okay. Fabric straight . . . and don't let it get bunched up," Gabe muttered to himself. "Got it."

He sat down in front of the machine and got started. Within a minute, the fabric caught around the needle, and it was all a big mess.

"It looks so easy when you do it," complained Gabe.

"You have to guide it with your hands and go at an even speed," Zoey explained, untangling the mess and smoothing out the fabric. "Here, try again."

"Can't you do it?" Gabe pleaded. "You're so much better at this than me."

"Helping is one thing, but I don't think it's right for me to do it for you," Zoey said. "Come on, Gabe! Embrace your inner tailor! When you're done, we can make brownies and chocolate chip cookies for Libby's bake sale." Zoey was grateful that even though Marcus had polished off the last bag of chocolate chips, their dad had restocked the baking supplies.

"Cookies? Now you're speaking my language," Gabe said. "Cookies, I can make."

"Not until you've finished the apron," warned Zoey. "That's what you came over here to do."

"Man, you're tough." Gabe sighed. "Okay, sewing a straight seam, take two."

Things went much better on his second try. It wasn't long before he'd finished the seams on all his pieces, and then Zoey showed him how to pin and sew them together.

"I need to do something extra for the competition," Gabe said. "What do you think about putting in an extra row of pockets for kitchen utensils? Maybe I could make it look like a tool belt or something."

"You've got enough fabric left over," Zoey said. "You can fold a long piece in half lengthwise and then sew vertical seams to make the pockets. If you sew it to the apron's waistline, it'll look a lot like a tool belt!"

Gabe cut the fabric, folded it in half, and sewed the pockets, while Zoey looked on and gave pointers. When he was done, Gabe put the apron on and modeled it.

"So? What do you think?"

"I think it's totally *tool*!" Zoey said, making Gabe laugh. "And it's time to do some baking . . . now that you're dressed for the occasion."

"Music to my ears," Gabe said.

Since Gabe was confident about his cookie-making skills, he took on that job while Zoey made brownies.

"I know my apron is nothing special," Gabe said while he measured out the flour, "but doing this project gave me a whole new appreciation for the amazing outfits you make, Zo."

"Thanks," Zoey said, feeling herself blush. She turned away to get some cookie sheets out of a drawer. "Let's get these cookies finished, so we can quality test the samples before your mom comes."

"Yes! We can't sell cookies without trying them first!" Gabe agreed. "If that isn't a law, it should be."

Saturday dawned crisp, cool, and sunny—perfect weather for the football game and Libby's bake sale. Mr. Webber drove Kate and Zoey, along with their plastic containers filled with treats, to the high school.

"Good luck!" he said as they got out of the car. "Hope you raise lots of money."

"Me too," Kate said. "The food pantry could really use a new fridge."

Libby and her dad had already set up the table and covered it with a gingham tablecloth. They had a hand-lettered sign saying that all proceeds were going to the food pantry. Libby wore an adorable, frilly apron over her dress, and she was busy arranging cakes and cupcakes.

"Wow, where did you get all these?" Zoey asked.

"Mom and I have been baking up a storm," Libby said. "But she couldn't come to help today because she has to take Sophie to a birthday party."

"And they wouldn't let me try anything unless I made a donation!" Mr. Flynn complained.

"*Dad*, I told you they're for charity!" Libby protested. "This is a fund-raiser, remember?"

Zoey felt bad about having eaten some cookie samples with Gabe. Oh well. She'd buy something extra to make up for it, she decided.

"I've got snickerdoodles, lots of superdelicious snickerdoodley doodles!" Priti announced when she arrived a few minutes later. "Oh, and yummy red velvet cupcakes, too."

"I'm glad I didn't have breakfast," Kate said. "I want to try everything!"

"Where's Libby?" Priti asked.

"I'm here!" Libby crawled out from under the table, where she'd been organizing the cake and cookie containers.

"I love your outfit, Libby," Priti said. "It's so cute for running a bake sale."

"Mom had this apron in a drawer—it seemed like a fun addition," Libby said.

Zoey noticed Kate look down at her striped

T-shirt and jeans. Kate looked like her usual, sporty-but-gorgeous self, but Zoey got the impression that Kate was having second thoughts about her outfit. She wondered if there was something going on between her two friends that she didn't know about, something that had made Kate change her mind about her dress for Libby's Bat Mitzvah.

"Hi, guys! Are you open for business yet?" Gabe surveyed the baked goods with his girlfriend, Josie. "I want to buy Josie some of the *magnifique* sweets Zoey and I made."

Gabe ended up buying cookies and brownies and some of Priti's snickerdoodles before heading to the bleachers.

The bake sale table did brisk business throughout the game. Tyler, who volunteered with Libby and Kate at the food pantry, came to stock up on snacks for his family before the halftime rush.

So this is the famous Tyler! Zoey thought.

Kate introduced him to Priti and Zoey. Zoey and Tyler said hi and then stood there awkwardly, each of them thinking about how their previous e-mail interactions had almost ruined things with Kate.

But then Kate made a joke of it. "It probably feels like you already know each other, right?" she said.

Tyler smiled. "Kind of."

"A little," Zoey said. "But I'm not going to interfere anymore!"

"He's cuter in real life than he was in the pictures," Priti whispered to Zoey. "Kate should definitely give him another chance!"

"I figured I'd stop by before you sell out of the good stuff," Tyler said. "I'm not used to coming to football games—I really came to support you guys—but if they have bake sales like this, maybe I'll come more often!"

"Oh, that's so sweet," Libby said. "Thanks, Tyler. I really appreciate it."

"It's cool you're doing this for the food pantry," Tyler said. "Pretty dress, by the way."

Zoey saw Kate's face fall when she heard Tyler compliment Libby on her dress. *Now* she was sure there was something specific that had made Kate change her mind about wanting a floral dress—and it wasn't just about wanting a change of pace. Zoey was about to suggest a trip to the restroom, so she could talk to Kate about her suspicions, when she caught sight of Allie.

"That's strange," Zoey said.

"What's strange?" Priti prompted.

"I just saw Allie going into the stands."

"Why is that strange?" Kate asked.

"Because she doesn't even like football," Zoey explained. "She was always pretty reluctant when Marcus asked her to come to the Eastern State games with us. I mean, she did, but she spent most of the time looking at fashion blogs on her phone and talking to me, not watching the game."

"That *is* weird," Priti agreed. "Something's not adding up. I wonder if she's here with the person she was texting."

"I don't know," Zoey said. "Do you think I should tell Marcus?"

"You can say you saw her at the game," Kate said. "That's just reporting a fact."

"I guess," Zoey said.

But she didn't have much time to think about

what to do, because halftime started, and the bake sale table was mobbed.

When the third quarter began, and things calmed down, Mr. Flynn said he was going to go watch the rest of the game.

"You girls seem to have everything under control," he said.

"And we don't have that much left to sell," Libby said, observing the now mostly bare table. "But come back before the end of fourth quarter to help us pack up."

Once her dad walked away, Libby launched into complaints about her mother.

"She's being *so unreasonable!*" Libby said. "She still won't budge on my Bat Mitzvah dress design, even though Aunt Lexie called and tried to persuade her. You know what she said to me after Aunt Lexie called?"

"What?" Zoey asked.

"She said, 'Nice try!' Can you *believe* that? It's totally unfair!" Libby twisted the end of her apron string into a tight knot. "So many other girls have worn strapless dresses. Why can't I?"

"That stinks," Priti said. "I know what it's like when your parents don't approve of your outfits. Remember how *my* parents were when I first started wearing black a lot?"

"Do you want me to come up with another design?" Zoey asked. "It's no problem, really. I should start figuring out something soon, though, because I still have to make the dress."

"Can you wait till tomorrow before you scrap the design?" Libby asked. "Aunt Lexie's coming to visit, and I'm hoping she'll work on Mom some more and change her mind."

"Oh cool! Tell her I say hi," Zoey said. She'd spent time with Aunt Lexie in New York and thought Libby's aunt was awesome. Almost as cool as Aunt Lulu . . . which was saying something!

"Zoey!" Libby said, grasping her friend's hands. "You should come over tomorrow!"

"I don't know . . . ," Zoey said. She definitely wanted to see Libby's aunt, but she didn't want to be there for another dress discussion. It was awkward enough the first time!

"You have to come, for moral support. *Pleeeease!*"

"Okay," Zoey agreed, hoping she hadn't made the wrong decision.

By the time Mr. Flynn came to help pack up, they'd sold out of everything except for one red velvet cupcake, which they gave to him as a thank-you.

Libby counted up all the money. "We raised three hundred and seventy-four dollars."

"That's great!" Priti exclaimed.

"It is," Kate agreed. "I figured we'd raise maybe two hundred, max. That's the most we've ever raised at a swim team bake sale."

"I know we did well," Libby said, sighing, "but it's not nearly enough for a commercial fridge."

"Rome wasn't built in a day, honey," Mr. Flynn said, giving her a quick hug. "I'm sure you'll get some money as gifts for your Bat Mitzvah that you can put toward the cost."

"I don't know if I want to give all my gift money," Libby said. "Just part of it. Is that selfish?"

"Not at all," Mr. Flynn replied. "You've been working so hard."

"We'll help you think of some other fund-raising ideas," Priti offered.

"Would you?" Libby asked. "I've just got so much other stuff to do to get ready for the big day, I'm starting to panic a little."

"Don't panic," Zoey said. "Helping out in a crunch is what friends are for."

When Dad dropped Zoey off at Libby's house the following day, Aunt Lexie had already arrived and was sitting at the kitchen table having a cup of coffee with Libby's mom.

"Zoey!" Aunt Lexie said, getting up to give her a hug. "It's so great to see you! We were just discussing the adorable dress you designed for Libby's Bat Mitzvah."

She winked at Zoey with her back to Mrs. Flynn.

"Oh . . . ," Zoey said. "How's that . . . um . . . going?"

"I agree that it's adorable, Zoey," Mrs. Flynn said. "Just not for Libby's Bat Mitzvah."

Libby, who'd just walked into the kitchen with Sophie, overheard her mother's comment and whined, "But *Mooooom* . . ."

"It's just not appropriate, honey," Mrs. Flynn

said. She got up and went over to the counter, where she fished out something from a pile of papers and came back to the table. "Look. I dug out a picture from my Bat Mitzvah. See how my shoulders are covered up and the neckline isn't too low?"

Libby, Zoey, Sophie, and Aunt Lexie all leaned over to look at the picture.

"Yes, sweetie, but look at how *short* it was," Aunt Lexie said, pointing to the hemline.

"Miniskirts were in style then," Mrs. Flynn said. "Boy, Mom and I had some fights about that. . . . I'd fallen in love with that dress, but she was dead set against me buying it. She finally gave in because her friends convinced her that it was the fashion. . . . What?"

She looked around the table and realized Aunt Lexie, Libby, and Zoey were all looking at her, grinning, and suddenly it dawned on her.

"Oh my goodness . . . I've turned into Mom, haven't I?" she exclaimed.

Aunt Lexie nodded, smiling lovingly.

"Yes, sister dearest, I'm afraid you have." She hugged Mrs. Flynn and said, "Don't worry. It's like they say, history repeats itself. Libby, you're giving your mom a hard time about what to wear just like your mom gave your grandma a hard time."

Libby looked at Zoey. Zoey smiled at Libby. At the very same moment, they broke out singing "Tradition," one of the songs they loved from *Fiddler on the Roof*.

Mrs. Flynn laughed. "I'm going to call Mom and apologize. Now that I have a twelve-year-old girl of my own, I understand where she was coming from."

She smiled at Libby. "Honey, when you have a twelve-year-old girl of *your* own who wants to wear something you don't approve of, I expect a phone call from you—and a *very* nice apology!"

Libby smiled at her mom while giving a side glance to Zoey.

"So can I wear the dress?"

Mrs. Flynn hesitated. "I'm still not crazy about it being strapless. I know it's the fashion, but I just . . ."

"I've got an idea," Zoey said. "How about I add some pretty off-the-shoulder, or cap sleeves, so it isn't quite strapless?"

"You could also modify the sweetheart neckline a bit," Aunt Lexie suggested. "Make it a very shallow dip in the middle, just for shape, though this dress sounds so pretty, you may not need the sweetheart neckline in the end."

"That would definitely be better," Mrs. Flynn said. "What do you think, honey?"

Zoey looked at her friend and nodded slightly, urging her to compromise with her mother.

"I can live with that," Libby said.

Mrs. Flynn added, "I still think she needs some sort of cover up—especially for the family photos."

"I can make a matching shrug," Zoey suggested. "That will give a little more coverage."

"Sounds like a perfect solution to me," said Aunt Lexie.

"Okay. Problem solved!" Mrs. Flynn said. "Until it's Sophie's turn."

"I want Zoey to design my Bat Mitzvah dress too!" Sophie piped up.

"Definitely," Zoey said. "I promise!"

------------ CHAPTER 6 ------------

In a *Flap* Over a Dress!

"Flap" is another word for "panic," which I just learned in English class. And *whew*! I'm happy to say that the Bat Mitzvah dress *flap* is over (though my panic about sewing the dress is just beginning)! Libby's mom thought it was too grown-up, but then Libby's aunt reminded her about Mrs. Flynn's own Bat Mitzvah, way back when: Libby's mom fought with her own mother about her Bat Mitzvah dress and was eventually allowed to wear it!

So, with a few changes, Libby and her mom finally agreed on a design, and now that everyone is satisfied with the compromise, I've been sewing like crazy.

If my mom were still alive, I wonder if we'd ever argue about clothes. It's hard to imagine that we'd argue about anything, but that's probably not realistic! Next time I video chat with Grandma Dorothy, I'm going to ask her what kind of outfits they argued about when Mom was young. I wonder if Mom would like the dress I designed for myself, or if she'd think it was too grown-up. . . .

Everything comes full circle. Maybe that's how it's supposed to be. . . . Still, I'm glad we managed to compromise on a design for Libby's outfit that makes everyone happy!

Now that Libby's dress situation was resolved to everyone's satisfaction, Zoey realized she had to tackle the topic of Kate's sudden desire to go floral. She'd put off starting on Kate's dress as long as possible, because she was afraid Kate would change her mind and want the circle pattern again. But time was running out, even though Kate's dress was a simple, relatively easy-to-make design.

"So, are you still thinking floral for your dress?" she asked Kate on the bus on Monday morning.

"I . . . think so," Kate said.

"You don't sound totally sure," Zoey said, thinking about Kate's reaction to Tyler complimenting Libby at the bake sale. "Do you mind me asking . . . does this have anything to do with Tyler?"

Kate stared at her. "How did you know? Did he talk to you?"

"NO!" Zoey exclaimed, not wanting Kate to think she'd been meddling in her love life again. "It was just . . . the look on your face when he complimented Libby on her dress at the football game."

"Oh . . . ," Kate said. Then she looked out the window.

"Well . . . *does* it have to do with him?"

"Yes," Kate confessed, turning back to Zoey. "I'm

so confused. At first he seemed to like that I was sporty. But now he seems to always be encouraging me to be more feminine—and he's constantly complimenting Libby on the way she dresses. Like at the game the other day, and when she wore that floral romper to volunteer at the food pantry last week."

"Has he said anything to you directly?" Zoey asked.

"Oh yeah, he's done that, too," Kate said. "He asks me why I don't wear skirts more often."

"He sounds like your mom!" Zoey laughed.

"I know, right?" Kate groaned. "She's always nagging me to pay more attention to girl stuff." She sighed. "I don't want to change just so Tyler likes me. But I've kind of been thinking. . . . I've always been so focused on sports all the time. . . . Maybe Mom's right. Maybe it wouldn't be so bad to try embracing my inner girl a little bit."

"You have to do it because you want to, not because Tyler or your mom wants you to," Zoey said.

"I *do* want to try being a little more girly," Kate said. "So I thought maybe adding flowers to my Bat

Mitzvah dress might be a way to start, especially because Tyler's always telling Libby he likes her flowery outfits."

"Well, it's totally your decision—but if that's really what you want, I could add some bold graphic flowers, more like silhouettes, which I think is more you than the little dainty flowers that Libby wears."

"That sounds great!" Kate said. "I don't know how you do it, Zo. You always know how to solve problems."

"Yeah, *other people's* problems," Zoey said as the bus pulled up in front of Mapleton Prep. "My own—not so much!"

"Well, thanks for solving mine, anyway."

"Just don't forget, Kate—if Tyler doesn't like you the way you are, then maybe he isn't the right guy for you," Zoey said. "Wow. I'm starting to sound like Dad."

Kate laughed. "We'll just have to see how things go, but point taken."

With less than a week to go before Libby's big day, Zoey spent that evening and the next one working on the dresses for her friends. After having to leave Libby's and Kate's till the last minute, she worried about getting her own finished in time.

Maybe I should just go in tuxedo pants for a little variety after sewing all these dresses, she thought as she worked on Libby's shrug. Daphne Shaw had posted a really cool woman's tuxedo on her blog. She'd worn it to an auction where she'd donated some of her fashions to help raise money. It was a fun idea, but Zoey decided she was too excited about her dress to wear a tuxedo.

Zoey looked up from the shrug she was working on toward where Libby's finished dress was adorning Marie Antoinette, Zoey's dress form.

"That's it!" she exclaimed. "I know how she can raise the money!"

She looked at the clock. It was too late to call her friend. She'd just have to wait until the next day to discuss her latest brainwave!

"So, I thought, after your Bat Mitzvah, we could auction off your dress to raise the rest of the money for the fridge," Zoey suggested to Libby the next morning before school. "I could write a post on my blog. I'm pretty sure we could raise a lot that way."

"Oh," Libby said. She didn't seem at all excited about the plan. In fact, she seemed distinctly unenthusiastic.

"What's the matter?" Zoey asked. "You don't like the idea?"

"No, it's a great *idea*," Libby said. "And I feel like kind of a jerk—like I'm really selfish for not wanting to do it. But I fought so hard to get Mom to agree to the design for that dress. I don't want think about giving it up before I've even tried it on."

"Well, you get to do that later when you come over for the fitting," Zoey said. "Besides, do you really see yourself wearing it again?"

"I don't know." Libby sighed. "It's just that I feel like my Bat Mitzvah is the first time I get to be a queen for a day, and the dress is part of what's going to make me feel really special. Do you hate me?"

"Of course I don't hate you!" Zoey said. "I'm sure we can think of another way to raise money."

"I hope so," Libby said.

Zoey and Priti were brainstorming ideas as they walked behind Emily and Ivy into industrial arts class.

"Did you see my new bracelets?" Emily asked, showing Ivy her wrist. She was wearing a stack of multicolored woven bracelets.

"They're fab!" Ivy said. "You've got *so many*."

"You can't have too much of a good thing, right?" Emily said.

"Can I see?" Zoey asked.

Emily stuck out her arm, and Zoey looked at the woven bracelets closely. They were pretty. But each one was at least ten dollars. She'd seen them in the "Hot Trends" section in the last issue of *Très Chic*. Emily must have had at least sixty dollars' worth on her wrist.

"Those are so cute!" Priti said. "Where did you get them?"

"At Boho Chic," Emily said. "On Main Street."

Zoey knew the store, but it wasn't somewhere she and her friends shopped. It was pricey.

"Where's yours, Ivy?" Emily asked. "You said you were going to get one, too."

"Oh . . . yeah. I am . . . I just haven't had time to go shopping. Both my parents are really busy with work and stuff . . . so . . . you know."

"But—"

Mr. Weldon cut off whatever Emily was about to say. "Okay, ladies, can we have a little less conversing and a little more focus on your projects? You can socialize at lunch."

Under his watchful eye, the girls got to work on their projects.

"Is it my imagination or did Ivy look like she'd just been saved by the bell?" Zoey whispered to Priti as she burned designs onto the wooden bow tie she was making for her friend Sean Wachikowski to wear to Libby's Bat Mitzvah.

"You mean saved by the teacher?" Priti muttered. "Definitely."

"What do you think of the bow tie?" Zoey said, holding it at her throat.

"What's not to love about a wooden bow tie?" Priti replied. "Sean is going to freak out."

"That's really cool," Ivy said. "Did you say it's for Sean?"

"Yes," Zoey said. "To wear to Libby's Bat Mitzvah."

"I bet Sean will love it," Ivy said. "The stripe design is really cool, and you can still see the wood grain."

"Thanks," Zoey said. "I'm almost finished. I made this belt, too," Zoey added, pointing at the wooden belt around her waist.

"You should come to the Fashion Fun Club meeting tomorrow to give it to him," Ivy suggested. "And, Priti, you can show everyone the necklace you're making out of wood pieces. Emily, you can wear the chopstick hair thingie you made. We could do a mini-industrial arts fashion show!"

"That would be fun!" Zoey said. She didn't like being a club leader when she had too many other things on her plate already, but going as a guest for a industrial arts fashion show sounded perfect.

"I don't think so," Emily said. "Zoey was kicked out of the Fashion Fun Club for a reason."

"I thought Sean said that Zoey could stop by the Fashion Fun Club anytime?" Priti said, remembering what Zoey had told her about how things ended.

Ivy opened her mouth, and for a moment Zoey

thought that she would actually challenge Emily to let Zoey come to the club meeting, just this once. But she didn't. Instead, she closed her mouth and shrugged, avoiding Zoey's gaze.

"It's probably better if I don't make such a big deal of the present, anyway," Zoey said, trying to make light of her disappointment.

"Sean will love it no matter where and when you give it to him," Priti said, giving Emily a pointed look. "It's really cool."

As Zoey picked up the wood burning tool to finish her design, she hoped Priti was right. Why did she suddenly start to doubt if Sean would like it all?

The next morning, Zoey found Sean at his locker, and she handed him a cute little paper bag filled with tissue paper.

"Hey, Sean. I've got a present for you."

"For *moi*?" Sean said. "But . . . what's the occasion? It's not my birthday." He thought for a moment. "Or even my halfbirthday."

"It's a present for no reason," Zoey said. "Because you're my friend."

Sean smiled. "Aw, that's the best kind of present of all. The suspense is killing me!"

He reached into the bag and found the wooden bow tie nestled amid all the tissue paper. "*Oh my gosh!* I looooove it!" he exclaimed. "Did you make this?"

"I did," Zoey said. "In woodshop. For you to wear to Libby's Bat Mitzvah."

"I'm going to rework my whole outfit around it," Sean said. "It's amazing."

"What's really amazing is that I managed to make your bow tie *and* a belt without losing any fingers or toes," Zoey said.

"You can use a band saw with your foot?" Sean asked. "Now *that's* something worth getting on video and putting online!"

"No, silly. But I could drop a trim saw on my toe."

"True." Sean held the bow tie up to his neck. "What do you think?"

"It's totally you." Zoey laughed.

"Thanks!" Sean said. "Can't wait to wear it this weekend!"

"I'm getting really excited for the party," Zoey told her friends at lunch.

"Glad someone's excited!" Libby groaned. "The main thing I'm looking forward to is being done with it . . . and wearing my party dress, of course."

"Thanks again for our dresses, Zoey," Kate said.

"You're very welcome," Zoey said. "But I'm feeling like Libby and am mostly relieved they're all done, including mine!"

"Well, I think it's cool that no one will be wearing Sew Zoey but us!" Priti said. "Emily probably *wishes* she could have one of your dresses."

"You know what's weird?" Zoey told her friends. "I'm starting to think it would almost be better if *Ivy* were coming to the party instead of Emily."

Priti had seen the more friendly side of Ivy lately, but Libby and Kate stared at Zoey like she had amnesia about how mean Ivy had been to Zoey in the past. "Who are you and what have you done with Zoey?" Kate asked.

"I know it's surprising," Zoey said, "but she seems different. Maybe people change."

CHAPTER 7

Flower Power

It's hard enough figuring out who you are and what's your best style. But then there's other people making comments about how you should dress. Parents, friends . . . and sometimes even boys. Is it possible to please everyone, including yourself? I reimagined the original dress I posted for Kate with graphic flower silhouettes so that she'll be happy with it—feminine but still comfortable. And, most important, still feel like herself.

The Bat Mitzvah is this weekend. I'm so excited for Libby's big day, especially after all the hard work she's been putting into it. I'm also looking forward to seeing my friends in the dresses I've been working so hard to make for them! Not to mention Sean in the wooden bow tie I made for him. He loved it! Whew! ☺

"I'm so nervous!" Libby confessed on Friday after school. "I haven't been able to concentrate all day!"

"Aren't you excited, too?" Priti asked. "I know I am. We're going to have so much fun tomorrow."

"I *am* excited. But first I have to get through the service without making any mistakes, and then I have to give a speech," Libby said. "We have all these friends and relatives arriving from out of town tonight—some of them are cousins I haven't seen in, like, *forever*."

"You're going to be fine, Libby," Kate said. "Even if you do make a mistake, I bet you wouldn't be the first one to do that. And think of how much this means to your grandfather."

"Definitely," Zoey agreed.

"You're going to be more than fine," Priti assured Libby. "You're going to be totally awesome."

"Thanks." Libby sighed. "I hope you're right!"

"Well, we'll be there cheering for you, even if you *do* mess up," Zoey said. "So try to stop worrying so much. Don't forget, you have a cute dress and a fun party to look forward to when the service is over."

Mrs. Mackey arrived bright and early to pick up Zoey for the Bat Mitzvah. The girls wanted to make sure they were there with plenty of time to spare, to give Libby moral support in case she was having any last-minute jitters.

"You look lovely," Mrs. Mackey said when Zoey got into the car. "And I just adore the dress you made for Kate to wear to the party tonight. I've been trying to get her into something floral and feminine for years and all I ever got was 'No way, Mom! Not my style.' Suddenly, she changes her mind!"

Kate crossed her arms and gave her mom a look.

"Don't get too excited, Mom. It's just a dress!"

Zoey had to agree with Mrs. Mackey. When Kate came to pick up the dress, she tried it on to make sure it fit properly and it really did suit her. The graphic flowers were feminine but still clean and simple and totally Kate.

"Your mom's right, you know," Zoey told Kate when they arrived at the synagogue. "You really *do* look great in the flower dress."

"Thanks," Kate said. "I *feel* good in it too, and I really appreciate you making it for me. I can't wait to wear it. But between us, I just don't want to give Mom any encouragement, or she'll go totally overboard. The next thing you know, she'll throw out all my jeans and T-shirts, and my closet will be filled with even more pink, frilly, flowery things I don't want."

Zoey laughed. "Come on, Kate, she's not *that* bad."

"That's what *you* think," Kate said. "I'm telling you, her dream is to see me dressed head to toe in pink for the rest of my life."

"Maybe just head to waist," Zoey admitted,

patting Kate's shoulder. "I'll give you that."

"That's bad enough," Kate groaned.

She was spared any further contemplation of a pink-clothed future by Priti's arrival.

"Now that we're all here, let's go inside and see how Libby is doing," Kate said. "Hopefully, she isn't too nervous."

Libby was in the synagogue lobby with her family, greeting friends and family. To the best friends who knew her so well, her cheeks were pale, and she looked very nervous behind her friendly, polite smiles.

When she saw the girls, her face lit up.

"Just need to use the restroom before the service," she told her parents as she came over to her friends. "Come with me, you guys?"

As soon as the door of the ladies room closed behind them, Libby confessed, "Actually, I don't have to go. I needed to get away for a pep talk. I'm scared to death to be the center of attention and to have to give a speech."

"You're going to be great," Priti assured her.

"Take a deep breath," Zoey suggested.

"Take *lots* of deep breaths," Kate said. "Breathe in and out slowly. We'll all do it together. Okay, here we go. . . . In . . . two . . . three. . . . Out . . . two . . . three."

They practiced slow breathing for a minute or two until the color came back into Libby's cheeks.

"I feel a little better," she said.

"You're going to be great," Zoey said. "You've been practicing this for, like, ever. You know it."

"And we're going to sit in the front row and be your cheerleaders," Priti said.

"You can't sit in the front row—my extended family is so big, they filled it up," Libby said.

"Okay, the second row," Kate said. "But you'll be able to see us, and we'll be smiling at you, so you'll know how awesome you are."

"That's right," Zoey agreed. "In fact, don't look up because you might get blinded by our teeth."

Libby laughed and then gave each of her friends a hug.

"You guys are the best. Now, I'd better get out there or my parents are going to send in a search party!"

Mrs. Flynn had saved seats for the girls, right behind the family.

"Libby asked that you sit right here," she said. "She wants to make sure she can see you."

Sophie swiveled around in her seat.

"Hi, Zoey! I love your dress. Did you make it?"

"I did," Zoey said.

"I can't wait till it's my Bat Mitzvah, so you can make *my* dress," Sophie said. "I want it to be just like Libby's, but even more prettier!"

Zoey laughed. "That's a tall order, Sophie, but luckily, I've got a while to think about it."

When the service began, Zoey was surprised by how much of it Libby conducted herself, even though the rabbi was standing by Libby's side. She was impressed by how calm and in control of everything her friend was, considering how anxious she'd been in the ladies' room just a half hour earlier.

Whenever Libby looked up, Zoey made sure she was smiling encouragingly, and once, she noticed the corner of Libby's mouth curl into an answering grin as her eyes returned to the prayer book.

If Libby made any mistakes with the Hebrew, Zoey certainly didn't know, but Libby's family nodded approvingly the entire time. When Libby finished reading from the Torah, her grandfather took out a handkerchief and wiped his eyes, smiling proudly through his tears.

Then Libby stood at the podium alone to make her speech. She talked about the passage she'd just read from the Torah, and how she related it to her life, and thanked her grandfather for inspiring her to have a Bat Mitzvah in the first place. Then she thanked her parents and sister, and her extended family. "And a final thank-you to my best friends—Kate, Priti, and Zoey—for helping me stay calm—well, *calmish*—when I was freaking out."

Finally, the service was over, and they gathered in the social hall to make a blessing on the bread and wine, and to have a little snack—bagels, fruit, and little pastries that Libby said were called rugelach—before the big celebration later in the evening. Libby told them this ceremonial blessing part was called the "kiddush."

"There's so much food!" Zoey exclaimed. "I thought you said it was just going to be a little snack."

"Mom might not be that religious, but she said she believes in the tradition of a big buffet, so no one goes hungry!" Libby said. "Luckily, we can donate the leftovers to the food pantry."

"That's great," Kate said. "I'm glad it won't go to waste."

"I'm just so relieved!" Libby said as they waited for the rabbi to say the blessing over the wine—or in their case, the grape juice. "Now I can finally relax and enjoy myself!"

"That's right," Priti said. "I can't wait till later. Time to P-A-R-T-Y!"

The rabbi recited the blessing, and they all clinked their tiny plastic glasses of grape juice.

"To Libby!" Zoey said.

"To celebrating!" Kate said.

They all took a sip. Then Libby's grandfather recited a blessing in Hebrew over the huge loaf of braided bread, which Libby told them was called "challah."

"Now, let's get some of those rugelach before they all disappear," Libby said. "I was too nervous to eat much this morning, and I'm *starving*!"

Later that evening, Mr. Webber drove Kate, Priti, and Zoey to Libby's Bat Mitzvah party.

"Have you ever been to Hilldown Manor?" Zoey asked her dad, looking at the address on Libby's invitation.

"I went to an alumni fund-raising event there once," Mr. Webber said.

"What's it like?" Kate asked.

"Nice," Mr. Webber said. "Pretty fancy. Big fountain out front. Valet parking."

He smiled at Zoey.

"Behave yourselves, now, ladies. I don't want to hear about you jumping in the fountain or anything."

"*Daaaad!*" Zoey groaned.

"We wouldn't do that, Mr. Webber," Priti assured him. "I wouldn't want to ruin my dress!"

"Of course," Mr. Webber said. "Silly me!"

He turned down an avenue of linden trees,

which opened to an imposing stone mansion with a large fountain out front, illuminated by lights.

"Wow!" Kate said. "You weren't kidding when you said it was fancy."

"I can't wait to see the inside!" Priti said. "It looks almost as glittery as my dress."

Mr. Webber laughed.

"You all look beautiful," he said, pulling up in front of the entrance, where a few young valets in red shirts waited to park the cars. "Have a great time! I'll see you tomorrow."

The girls had arranged to have a sleepover in Libby's basement, so they could attend the close-family-and-friends brunch the following morning. They'd dropped clothes and pajamas at Libby's house earlier in the week.

They could hear the DJ as soon as they walked in. In the hallway, there were a few different photo backdrops, including one of a candy store, to go along with Libby's Bat Mitzvah theme.

"Let's take our picture!" Priti exclaimed.

The photographer let them choose from a big box of props. Zoey wrapped a big furry Twizzler across her shoulders, Kate held an enormous Jolly Rancher, and Priti wore a hat that looked like the top of a Pez dispenser.

"Say 'sweets'!" he said.

"SWEETS!" they chorused.

He printed out three copies of the picture, one for each of them. The photograph said "Libby's Bat Mitzvah Celebration" on the border.

"Wow, that's really *sweet*!" Priti said.

The girls took their photos and went to explore the rest of Hilldown Manor.

"Ooh, look, glow sticks!" Kate exclaimed, seeing a table with candy-decorated baskets filled with a variety of glowing fluorescent sticks and bendable strings outside the ballroom doors.

Kate and Zoey made glowing bracelets and necklaces. Priti went with a glowing crown and anklets.

"Now, I sparkle and glow from head to toe!" she said, twirling for her friends. "Let's *glow* to the dance floor!"

Libby was in the center of the dance floor, next to the party coordinator, who was starting up a Hula-Hoop competition. Libby's face lit up when she saw her friends. She looked beautiful in her dress. "You're here! Just in time!" she exclaimed.

Libby turned to the party coordinator, whose name was Alvin, and informed him that Kate was the Hula-Hoop queen of their group.

"Great!" Alvin said, grabbing a very embarrassed Kate by the hand and pulling her to the middle of the dance floor. He handed her a glowing Hula-Hoop. He took another one for himself and said to Kate, "Are you ready?"

Kate's face was flushed with embarrassment at being the center of attention, but she was a natural competitor. "I was born ready," she said.

"That's what I like to hear," Alvin said. "Okay, Frank the DJ, hit it!"

At the first strains of "Twist and Shout," they were off. Alvin was a flashy hooper with style galore, but Kate had the edge on stamina.

"Oh, look, Miles is here!" Priti said in Zoey's ear as they watched the contest.

"Ugh, and there's Emily," Zoey said, catching sight of the person she least wanted to see on the other side of the dance floor.

Alvin's hoop finally fell to his ankles, and he raised Kate's arm and proclaimed her the victor with a necklace made of candy.

"Now, enjoy some of the fine eats and then come back here for some more games," he said.

"You guys are at my table, of course," Libby said, dragging them over to a big round table with a huge centerpiece made from different types of candy.

"Can we eat the centerpiece?" Priti asked.

"Someone at the table gets to take it home," Libby said. "That's if you're hungry after dessert. Have you seen the dessert table? There's a chocolate fountain."

"Can't we just skip dinner and go straight to dessert?" Zoey asked.

"I wish," Libby said.

There were already some kids sitting at their table, some of whom Zoey recognized—like Miles, Sean, Gabe, Josie, and Tyler.

Libby introduced them to friends from her Hebrew school class. Zoey couldn't help noticing that one, Ezra, was really cute. She whispered a question into Libby's ear, asking if he was nice.

"Ezra's really sweet," Libby whispered back.

Over the main course, they all introduced themselves, but mostly the Hebrew school kids talked to their classmates, and Libby's school friends talked to one another, with little intermingling.

Between courses, Alvin called them back to the dance floor.

"Now we're going to play an icebreaker game called Snowball. Can I have a volunteer? I'm giving away this top hat to the first one with their hand up!"

Zoey's hand shot straight into the air, because she thought the hat would top off her outfit to perfection. Alvin pulled her to the middle of the dance floor.

"What's your name?"

"Zoey."

"Thanks for volunteering, Zoey," he said, placing the top hat on her head.

Zoey loved it, and she planned to wear it all night.

"Now, all of you form a circle around Zoey and me," Alvin began. "And we're going to start off the dancing . . . then Frank the DJ is going to call out—"

"SNOWBALL!" shouted Frank the DJ.

"Then Zoey's going to pick a new partner, and so am I, and we're going to dance with our new partners until the next time Frank the DJ yells out—"

"SNOWBALL!" all the kids shouted with the DJ.

"You guys are quick," Alvin said. "I bet you get good grades in school. Okay, let's get this party started, Frank!"

As soon as the music started, Zoey and Alvin began to dance. But Zoey was worrying about who she should pick to dance when Frank the DJ said, "Snowball!" She wanted to ask Ezra, but would that be too weird since she didn't even know him? Except Alvin did say it was supposed to be an icebreaker, right?

"SNOWBALL!"

With no more time to think, Zoey turned to Ezra and pointed. He smiled and joined her on the dance floor.

"Nice hat!" Ezra said.

"Thanks," Zoey said. "So . . . you know Libby from Hebrew school?"

"That's right," Ezra said. "I know you know her from school because she talks about you and your other friends all the time."

He has a really, really *cute smile,* Zoey thought.

They only got to dance together for a short while before it was Snowball time again, but it was enough for Zoey to decide that Ezra was even cuter up close than he was from across the table.

She picked Sean next.

"Hey, I love your bow tie," she said.

"Me too!" Sean said, smiling. "This really cool friend of mine made it in woodshop!"

Soon the dance floor was full, and Zoey was having a great time dancing with different partners—boys she knew from school, and friends of Libby's from Hebrew school. But then Alvin announced it was the moment they'd all been waiting for . . . DESSERT!

"I can't choose! It all looks so yummy," Priti moaned when they reached the front of the mob at the dessert table. "I want to try *everything*!" She took a few pictures of the table with her cell phone. "Mom asked me to take pictures, so that I can describe all the desserts to her for her blog," she explained.

"I just want to try everything, period," Kate said.

"Well, I'm not impressed."

Zoey looked up to see who was talking and saw Emily, who was looking at the spread of goodies with a scornful expression.

"My mother's a chef, and her desserts put these to shame," Emily said. "This caterer is really lame."

Zoey glanced over at Libby to see if she'd heard, but fortunately she was busy chatting with other friends around the chocolate fountain.

"Well, I think the food has been amazing so far," Zoey said. "And these desserts look really superyummy."

"That makes two of us," Ezra agreed. He'd come to stand next to her in the dessert line, which made Zoey nervous and happy at the same time. "In fact, I'm going to grab two of these gooey brownie things before they're all gone."

Emily raised her chin and stomped away from the table.

"What got into her?" Sean asked, grabbing a

plate from the buffet and starting to load it with brownies, cookies, and cupcakes.

"She hasn't eaten enough sweets," Ezra said, joking.

"That's not going to be Sean's problem," Priti observed, eyeing Sean's full plate. "I'm going to explore the chocolate fountain."

She drifted toward the melted chocolate.

"Cool tie," Ezra said. "Is it made of wood?"

"Yeah," Sean said. "Zoey made it."

"You did?" Ezra asked Zoey. "Wow. That's so awesome."

Sean winked at Zoey. She wondered if it was obvious that she thought Ezra was cute, and she resolved to play it cool.

"Love the top hat, Zoey!" Sean said. "It makes the outfit."

Over the dessert course, Libby's two groups of friends were mingling more—switching seats and having fun getting to know one another.

"Emily is just plain wrong," Priti said after she'd tried every single dessert. "These taste as good or better than they look."

"Yeah, they're amazing," Ezra said. "Why was that girl so snarky about them?"

"Who, Emily?" Zoey said. "She's just . . . Well, her mom is a chef, so she's always comparing everything to how her mom does it."

Ezra looked dubious. "She's still a guest at this party, though, right? That was just rude. What if Libby heard?"

"'What if Libby heard what?'" Libby asked. She'd been flitting around the room saying hi to all her relatives and other guests. "Come on, it's time to dance again!"

She grabbed Sean's hand and dragged him to the dance floor. Tyler asked Kate to dance, and Priti asked Miles. Gabe and Josie were an automatic pair, of course.

Zoey watched her friends head off to the dance floor and was finishing up her dessert when she felt someone tap her on the shoulder.

"So . . . do you want to dance?" Ezra asked.

"Sure!" Zoey replied, thrilled that he'd asked her.

"I really like your dress," Ezra said. "It looks cool when you dance."

"That's 'cause it's a flapper dress," Zoey said. "Actually, I made it."

"For real?" Ezra exclaimed. "The bow tie *and* your dress?"

"And Libby's dress. And Kate's and Priti's, too!" Zoey said with a smile.

"I don't believe you. They're all so different," he said. "Plus, they look like they came from a real store!"

"The store of Sew Zoey—in my house," she joked, laughing.

"I feel so boring and underdressed now," Ezra said. "Hey, can I borrow your prize top hat?"

Zoey nodded, and he plucked it off her head and settled it on his own. He looked adorable.

She looked around to see if her friends noticed, and she overheard Tyler telling Kate that he liked all the flowers on Libby's dress.

"What about my dress? Do you like mine?" Kate asked.

"Well . . . yeah," Tyler said.

Kate didn't look happy with his response. Not one little bit. The two of them stopped dancing and started what looked like an intense conversation by the edge of the dance floor.

When the song ended, Alvin announced that it was time for the traditional hora. The older guests joined the younger ones on the dance floor, and everyone made a big circle along the edge.

Just then Kate came over to where Zoey was chatting with Ezra. She seemed upset.

"Zoey, can you come with me to the bathroom?"

"Sure," Zoey said, waving good-bye to Ezra.

Zoey was a little disappointed to miss the hora after all the practicing they'd done, but Kate needed her. The two girls headed off to the ladies' room.

"I'm sorry, Zo. I know you wanted to dance the hora, but I really need to talk," Kate said.

"Are you okay?" Zoey asked, although it was pretty clear Kate wasn't.

"I finally told Tyler that I don't appreciate how he's always talking about how much he likes all the really girly stuff Libby wears—how it makes me feel bad," Kate said. "Dressing like that just isn't my style. It's not who I am—at least not for now—and I want him to like me for who I am, not just for my clothes."

"What did he say?" Zoey asked.

"He said he was sorry—that he didn't mean to upset me. It's just that he really likes Libby's style. So then . . . Well, I said that if he likes Libby's style so much, why doesn't he just go out with Libby? Maybe they'd be a better match than him and me."

"Wow," Zoey said. "What did he say?"

"He said he really likes *me*, not Libby, and he'll try to be more considerate in the future."

"That's good, right?" Zoey said.

"I guess," Kate said. "But why did he compliment Libby's dress and not say a word about mine? I changed it to a floral pattern mostly because I thought he would like it. I mean, I came around to the idea too, and now I love it, but it started because of him."

"I don't know," Zoey confessed. "But . . . I think it's good you finally told him how you feel. And it sounds like he's going to try to be more aware of the things he says."

"You're right," Kate said. "Thanks."

Zoey gave her friend a hug. "Anytime," she said.

"Come on. Let's get back," Kate said. "Ezra still

has your top hat, which means you get another dance with him!"

When they got back to the reception, Alvin and his assistant party motivators were rolling out huge sheets of Bubble Wrap onto the dance floor.

"Are you ready to Snap, Crackle, and Pop?" Alvin asked when they were done.

"That looks like fun!" Zoey exclaimed to Kate. They joined Priti and Libby on the edge of the dance floor.

Just then she noticed Emily approach Ezra, who was standing by the dance floor, still wearing Zoey's top hat. Emily smiled at Ezra and tilted her head toward the Bubble Wrap. Ezra shrugged and then shook his head. Emily tossed her hair and walked away.

"Did you see that?" Priti exclaimed.

"Yeah," Zoey said. "I wonder what that was all about."

Then Priti nudged her with an elbow—Ezra was walking toward them.

He smiled and handed Zoey back her top hat.

"You probably want your prize back," he said. "It looks cuter on you, anyway."

Zoey felt herself blushing. She hoped it wasn't too obvious.

"Hey, you know that girl who just asked me to dance?" Ezra asked.

"Who, Emily?" Priti said.

"Yeah. The one who was complaining about all the desserts. What's her deal? Why is she so . . . complain-y?"

"I don't know." Zoey sighed. "She's like that at school, too."

"Well, let's not ruin our good time by talking about her, then," Ezra said. "Let's pop some bubbles instead!"

By the time the Bubble Wrap was flattened by dancing feet, Zoey and her friends were giggling and breathless. Frank the DJ kept the music upbeat, and it felt like they were at their own private club full of their favorite kids, with one exception. But even Emily seemed to be having a good time, despite all of her earlier complaining. Before the night was over, Libby grabbed Zoey, Priti, and Kate, and they took more pictures against the photo backdrops. It was the best Bat Mitzvah party ever, and they wanted to remember it!

But like all fun things, it came to an end. Frank the DJ had promised the older crowd a slow song. The younger set cleared the floor.

Mrs. Flynn came over to the table and kissed Libby.

"You look beautiful, honey. I'm so proud of you," she said.

"Thanks, Mom," Libby said.

"And, Zoey—I meant to find you earlier. Thank you for altering the design for Libby's dress," said Mrs. Flynn. "It looks fantastic. Everyone keeps asking me where we bought it."

"I'm just happy I could make a design everyone could agree on!" Zoey said.

Ezra got up and came to say good-bye and to thank Libby.

"I just got a text that my parents are waiting outside," he said. "I wish I could stay longer."

"I'm glad you could come," Libby said.

"It was great to meet you," Ezra told Zoey. "Maybe we'll see each other again sometime."

"Maybe," Zoey said. She definitely hoped so!

Because they were staying over at Libby's house, the girls were among the last to leave.

"That was the best party EVER!" Priti exclaimed as they left the hall, waving good-bye to Frank the DJ, who was packing up his equipment. "I wish everyone had Bat Mitzvahs!"

"I wish it didn't have to end." Libby sighed. "I spent so many months preparing and worrying about messing up, and now it's all over!"

"There's still the brunch tomorrow," Kate said, making Libby laugh.

Zoey was only half listening to her friends as they stood at the building's entrance, because she'd caught sight of something that didn't make sense: Allie. What was *she* doing here? She was standing in the parking lot, talking to one of the valets. Then the guy tucked a loose strand of hair behind Allie's ear, and she stroked his arm, making it pretty clear they weren't just friends—they were more than friends.

Zoey realized that he might be the person Allie had been texting when she and Allie had gone out for hot chocolate. Could Allie have broken up with Marcus because she was already interested in someone else? If so, Zoey concluded, it would mean Allie had lied to Marcus—and to Zoey—about her reasons for ending things.

"I'll be back in a minute," she said to her friends, who hadn't noticed Allie, and marched over to the couple.

"Hi, Allie—I didn't expect to see you here," Zoey said.

Allie turned around, shocked to see Zoey. She flushed bright red. "Oh . . . Hi, Zoey! I'm . . . here to give my . . . *friend* . . . Oliver a ride home," she said. "His car's in the shop."

The boy, Oliver, looked surprised. "Friend? Really? Is that all I am?"

Zoey didn't think it was possible for someone's face to get any redder, but Allie's did. That seemed to confirm that Allie hadn't been straight with her.

"I'm sorry. Zoey, this is Oliver. Oliver, this is my friend Zoey, Marcus's sister."

"You mean like Marcus, as in your ex?"

Allie nodded, looking distinctly uncomfortable.

"Wow," Oliver said.

"Exactly," Zoey agreed.

"Zoey, please don't tell Marcus I'm already seeing someone," Allie pleaded. "I really like Marcus. It's just . . . I met Oliver, and we get along really well . . . but the last thing I want to do is hurt Marcus."

Zoey was about to say, *Too late!* But she stopped herself just in time. Marcus would be mortified if Allie knew how upset he was, especially since she seemed to have wasted no time moving on to someone new.

"Hey, Zoey!" Priti called. "It's time to go!"

Sure enough, Mrs. Flynn's car was in front of the reception hall, and her friends were starting to pile in.

"Please, Zoey?" Allie asked again.

Zoey shrugged and ran to the car, her emotions churning.

"What was Allie doing here?" Priti asked.

"Yeah, I wasn't expecting to see her," Libby said.

Zoey looked at her friends, who were all flushed

and happy from having had such a wonderful time at the party. She didn't want to take away from the magical time they'd had by sharing the news of Allie's deception. So she decided to share only half the truth tonight.

"She's giving her friend Oliver a ride home because his car broke down," she said.

The real reason could wait.

--------- CHAPTER 8 ---------

Family Tree'ed

I'm not sure if I can keep track of all the Van Langen/ Flynn aunts and uncles and cousins who were at Libby's Bat Mitzvah yesterday. If I were Libby, I probably would have embarrassed myself by calling someone by the wrong name, but she did an amazing job, both with the service and with identifying her relatives! That made me wish everyone wore name tags, even though some people think they're dorky. Maybe it would be cooler if the whole dress was a name tag, like in the sketch?

Anyhoo, it was so cool that Libby's family came from all over to be there for her—cousins from California and Seattle traveled across the country to Mapleton. Libby's hoping that between what we raised from the bake sale and the portion of the gift money from her Bat Mitzvah guests, she'll have enough to buy the food pantry their new refrigerator. Keep your fingers crossed!

"Now this is what I call brunch!" Zoey said, surveying the Flynns' dining room table, which was laden with bagels, cream cheese, lox, egg salad, tuna fish, five different types of sliced cheese, blintzes, and an assortment of delicious-looking cookies and pastries.

"And here I thought it was just my mom who always makes too much food because she worries that one person might be hungry," Priti said. "There's enough food here to feed a small army!"

"Didn't you see all my relatives yesterday?" Libby joked. "There are so many of them, it *is* like a small army!"

Sure enough, once the family and out-of-town guests arrived, the food started disappearing pretty rapidly. Sophie was running around the house with her young cousins, having a wonderful time.

Zoey was almost enjoying herself enough to forget about what she'd discovered the previous evening . . . but it still kept nagging at the back of her mind.

"What's the matter, Zo?" Priti asked her quietly as they went to refill their drinks.

"What do you mean? Do I look like something is the matter?"

"Not to everyone," Priti said. "But this is *me* we're talking about. One of your BFFs. Come on, spill!"

Zoey sighed and then proceeded to explain the real story of what had happened with Allie and Oliver the previous evening.

"So, now I don't know what to do. Allie wanted me to promise not to tell Marcus, but he's my brother. How can I keep this a secret from him?"

"I don't know," Priti said, shaking her head. "This is a really tough situation."

"You can say that again." Zoey sighed. "Why did Marcus and Allie have to start going out in the first place?"

"I think we should ask Libby and Kate what they think," Priti said. "After all, four heads are better than two."

"But it's Libby's party," Zoey said. "I don't want to ruin it for her."

"You're not ruining it, silly. We're your friends," Priti said. "That's what we're here for."

Ignoring Zoey's protests, Priti called over Kate and Libby and then explained the situation to them.

"Wow," Kate said. "That's superawkward."

"Talk about being caught in the middle," Libby agreed.

"I know!" Zoey wailed. "What should I do? I was thinking about it so much last night I could barely sleep!"

"I don't know what say," Kate said. "This is out of my league."

"Mine too," Libby said. "But I know one thing: You shouldn't keep this a secret from Marcus, no matter what Allie says."

"Libby's right," Priti agreed. "If he finds out you knew and didn't tell him, he'll be really mad."

"But I don't want to be the one to tell him," Zoey said mournfully. "What if he ends up being mad at me? You know, shooting the messenger?"

"Good point," Libby said.

"Call Allie and tell her *she* has to tell Marcus," Kate said finally. "I mean, she keeps saying how much she cares about him, right?"

Zoey nodded.

"So if she means what she says, he deserves the real explanation of why she broke up with him, not some lame excuse," Priti said. "At least, I think that's what my older sisters would say."

"You're right," Zoey said. "I'm going to call her when I get home and tell her she has to come clean with Marcus. It's not fair of her to ask me to keep secrets from my brother."

She looked around at her friends and smiled.

"I feel so much better now we've figured out

what to do. But I think I need a cookie to make me feel one hundred percent back to normal."

Libby laughed. "Have you seen the amount of baked goods on the dining room table?" she asked. "I think that can be arranged!"

Later that afternoon, when she got back home, Zoey called Allie.

"Listen, I've decided not to tell Marcus. . . ."

"Oh, thanks," Allie said, sounding really relieved.

"But that's because I realized *you* need to tell him yourself," Zoey continued.

"Oh."

"You haven't been fair to him, Allie," Zoey said. "Even if he hadn't given you the ring and gotten all serious, you like someone else and would have broken up with him anyway. If you really care about him, you should be honest."

"But—"

"And besides, you've put me in a seriously awkward position," Zoey said. "We're friends, but you're asking me to lie to my brother. How is that fair? A good friend wouldn't do that."

There was silence on the line, and Zoey wondered if Allie had hung up on her.

"You're right, Zoey," Allie said finally. "I feel terrible. It's bad enough I've hurt Marcus by breaking up with him. I thought it would be easier on him if I didn't tell him I liked someone else, but maybe that was wrong. And now I've hurt you too, by asking you to lie to him."

It was good to hear Allie admit that. But Zoey wanted to make sure she was going to take action.

"So are you going to tell him?"

"I'll text him now and tell him we need to talk," Allie said. "And Zoey . . . I'm sorry. I really hope we can still be friends. I'd hate if a relationship with *any* boy came between us."

Marcus was more cheerful at breakfast than he'd been for days.

"What's up with you, sunshine?" Dad asked.

"Allie texted me last night," he said, practically bouncing around the kitchen. "She wants to meet to talk after school. I think it's a good sign. Maybe she wants to get back together."

Or not . . . , Zoey thought, her heart sinking. She hadn't thought that Marcus might get the wrong idea from Allie's text message.

"Maybe you shouldn't get your hopes up too much," she said. "Maybe she just wants to talk . . . you know, like as friends."

Marcus stopped pouring orange juice and gave her a look.

"Thanks, Debbie Downer. I'll keep that in mind."

"Zoey's right," Dad said. "Meet her assuming that she wants to stay just friends, and then you won't be setting yourself up for disappointment."

"Why are you guys so down on romance all of a sudden?" Marcus complained. "What makes you think I'm going to be disappointed?"

Zoey hadn't told her father about what she'd seen in the parking lot. Maybe he just had enough experience from his own dating life.

"I'm not down on romance, kiddo," Dad said. "I'll vote for romance any day of the week. But to borrow from Shakespeare: 'The course of true love never does run smooth.' I don't want you to get hurt."

Marcus chugged his orange juice and put his glass down on the counter a little more forcefully than usual.

"Well, if she didn't like me, she wouldn't want to get together. Right, Zoey?"

"I don't know." Zoey shrugged, feeling awful because she knew the real reason for the meeting. She picked up her backpack and headed for the door. "Good luck!"

Zoey was on pins and needles all day, worrying about how Marcus would react to Allie's revelations. Would he be even more miserable? Was he going to be mad at Zoey for not telling him right away about the run-in at the Bat Mitzvah? Hopefully, Allie wouldn't tell Marcus that Zoey knew about the other guy.

After school, she decided to make some of his favorite double chocolate chip cookies in case he was sad or mad, or both.

The first batch was just coming out of the oven when she heard the garage door open, and a few minutes later, Marcus came strolling in.

"Hey, something smells good."

He spotted the tray of cookies and nabbed one off the tray.

"Just what the doctor ordered!" he said.

"How did it go?" Zoey asked.

"Okay," Marcus said. "Except . . . why did you tell Allie I was doing just fine without her and getting really good on the guitar and practicing a lot with the band? She asked me to play her something new, and I had nothing to offer. Nada! I felt like a total jerk."

"But . . . you made me promise not to let her know that you were upset!" Zoey protested. "What was I supposed to do?"

"I don't know," Marcus admitted. "But when I told Allie the truth, about how upset I was, it came as a big surprise!"

"I'm a really bad liar," Zoey complained. "I didn't know what to do! Allie asked me how you were, and I was on the spot. I guess I should have just shrugged and said 'Okay' or something, but instead I made up the thing about the guitar just to have something to say. I had no idea that saying you were doing well would end up being as wrong as saying you were doing badly."

"Since you've made my favorite cookies, I'll try to forgive you," Marcus said, grabbing a second one and taking a bite. "Also, because even though it's still a bummer that Allie broke up with me, it's a relief to know it's really because she likes someone else, not because I put my heart on the line."

"So . . . you're over it?" Zoey asked.

"Not exactly *over* it," Marcus said, going to pour himself a glass of milk. "I'm still upset she broke up with me, and I'm mad she's already dating someone else. But in a way, it's kind of a relief, because if she broke up with me because she likes someone else, I don't have to keep wondering about what I did wrong."

"I guess that's one way of looking at it," Zoey said. As far as she was concerned, whatever way Marcus wanted to look at it that made him less mopey and miserable was fine with her!

"Dad always says, 'There's a lid for every pot,'" Marcus reminded Zoey, giving a pretty good imitation of their father. "I guess I'll be searching for a better-fitting lid. Though if Allie changes her mind, *maybe* I'll reconsider."

Zoey sighed. "Relationships seem so complicated. I mean, Uncle John and Aunt Lulu seem to get on really well and are in love and all that, but her first marriage ended in divorce—and Priti's parents ended up getting divorced too."

"And then there's Dad and the Mystery Lady, whom we never even get to meet," Marcus said. "They seem to get along, but who knows?"

"He better introduce us to her soon," Zoey grumbled.

"Definitely," Marcus agreed. "It's time for the Mystery Lady to be revealed."

The next day at lunch, Libby announced that she'd added up all her Bat Mitzvah money.

"If I give some of the gift money, plus the money from the bake sale, I'll have just over half of what I need to raise to buy the fridge," she said. "I thought about giving more of my Bat Mitzvah gift money, but my parents said they wanted me to save some for when I go to college—and to spend a little bit doing something fun, too, since I worked so hard."

"So what are you going to do to raise the rest?" Kate asked.

"Well, I've thought about it, and I realized that maybe Zoey was right," Libby said. "I mean, I had the most amazing time wearing my dress, and I felt incredibly special in it, but if I auction it off, some other girl could wear it and feel special *and* I'd raise more money for the food pantry's fridge. Maybe not the whole amount I need, but every bit helps."

"That's great!" Zoey said. "I bet you'll raise at least seventy-five dollars. Maybe more!"

"I just want to make sure it goes to another Bat Mitzvah girl," Libby said. "So that she can feel as special on her big day as I did. My parents said they'd send an e-mail to all the guests about the auction."

"Maybe you can put up a sign at your Hebrew school, too," Priti suggested.

"That's a good idea," Libby said. "Also, I was wondering, Zo . . . can you do a blog post?"

"Sure!" Zoey said. "I'd be happy to!"

"If I could finally raise enough money to donate

the fridge," Libby said, "that'll be the best Bat Mitzvah present of all."

"You'll do it," Kate said.

"Definitely!" Priti agreed.

"We are *so* going to make this happen!" Zoey said. They all raised their milk cartons to drink to the ultimate success of Libby's project.

════════ CHAPTER 9 ════════

Dream Dress for a Cause

Hey, Sew Zoey readers! I've got a special guest blog today from one of my BFFs, Libby. I'll let her explain!

Hi! I'm Libby! I just had my Bat Mitzvah, and for my mitzvah project, I created a kitchen garden to grow vegetables for the food pantry where I volunteer, so the people who come there can have healthy, fresh produce to supplement the canned and boxed food. But that also means the food pantry needs a new industrial fridge in order to properly store the fresh produce. What I'm able to grow isn't enough to fill the whole fridge regularly, but the head of the food pantry and I arranged for local farms to donate produce a few times a week. Thanks to help from my BFFs and my Bat Mitzvah guests, I've raised just over half the cost from a bake sale and from gifts. But I'm trying to raise the last bit I need—or at least part of it—by auctioning off my Bat Mitzvah dress. It's hard to let go of the dream dress that Zoey made for me, but if it gets a second life as another girl's dream dress—and helps provide delicious, healthy food (via the new refrigerator) for families who come to the food pantry—it will be worth it! Thanks for your help and support!

   XO, Libby

   Hi! It's me, Zoey, again. So we're trying to figure out the best way to auction the dress. Any suggestions?

When Zoey checked her blog the next day after school, there was a comment from her fashion mentor, Daphne Shaw.

Try Fundworthy.edu. It's a site where kids and schools can safely set up auctions to raise money for school clubs, events, and nonprofits. And they don't take a big percentage, unlike some of the other auction sites. Let me know when you set up your page, and I'll spread the word around the studio and on my blog.

Zoey called Libby right away to tell her.

"That's awesome!" Libby squealed. "If Daphne puts the auction on her blog, then maybe we'll be able to raise all the money!"

Zoey couldn't imagine that a dress she made would ever sell for that much, but she didn't want to discourage Libby.

"Well, first we have to set up the auction page," Zoey said. "Why don't you come over tomorrow night for a sleepover, and my dad can help us?

Then we can get the whole thing rolling."

"Sounds like a plan!" Libby said.

The following evening after dinner, Mr. Webber helped them set up the auction page.

"What do you want to call it?" he asked.

"Dream Dress for a Cause," Libby said.

"Okay," Mr. Webber said after he'd typed the name in. "And how long do you want the auction to run?"

"What do you think, Zoey?" Libby asked.

"How about a week?" Zoey suggested. "That's long enough to let people know about it, but not too long that we'll have to wait for weeks to find out."

"Sounds good," Dad said.

He uploaded several pictures of the dress on Marie Antoinette, and one of Libby wearing it. Mr. Webber cropped that photo so that Libby's face wasn't visible, for safety and privacy purposes.

"I think Libby should be the one to press the button to post this online," he said.

"I'm so nervous!" Libby said. "I hope this works!"

She pressed enter, and "Your Auction: Dream Dress for a Cause is now LIVE!" appeared on the screen.

"Now we just have to wait and see if we get some bids," Zoey said, refreshing the page to see if they had a bid yet. "That's the hard part."

"A watched pot never boils," Dad said, laughing when Zoey refreshed the page again. "Go do something else for a while!"

After watching a movie, accompanied by a bowl of popcorn, Zoey and Libby checked the auction page again.

"Look! There's a bid!" Libby exclaimed.

"It's only twenty-five dollars, but it's a start," Zoey said.

Sure enough, by the time they went to bed that night, two more bids had come in, bringing the total to sixty dollars.

"It's still a long way to go." Libby sighed. "Do you think we'll get there?"

"We've got a whole week of the auction left," Zoey said. "I'm going to post the link on my blog tomorrow morning. And don't forget, Daphne Shaw promised to spread the word around her studio and post about it on her blog. That will make a difference."

"I hope so," Libby said. "I have to make this fridge happen!"

Libby texted her friends updates throughout the weekend whenever new bids came in. By Sunday night, there were twenty bids, and it was up to one hundred and seventy-five dollars. By Monday at lunch, there were thirty-two bids with the highest bid at two hundred and sixty. But by Tuesday, the bids had slowed.

"There have only been two more bids since yesterday," Libby said. "And the price has only gone up to two hundred and seventy-five dollars. What happens if this is it? I still wouldn't have raised enough to buy the refrigerator."

"Let me see if Daphne posted about it yet," Zoey said. She checked Daphne's blog on her phone. "She hasn't. I'm sure when she does, you'll get more bids."

"But there's only a few days left," Libby said worriedly. "What if she's forgotten to do it?"

"I'm sure she won't," Zoey assured her.

But deep down, she wondered the same thing. At dinner, she asked her father if maybe she should write and ask Daphne why she hadn't posted it.

"Honey, Daphne Shaw is a very busy lady, and it's wonderful she's taken such an interest in you," Dad said. "It was really kind of her to offer to do you a favor, but you shouldn't bother her about it."

"What if she forgets?" Zoey asked.

"Then she forgets," Dad said. "But she hasn't let you down so far, has she?"

"No," Zoey admitted.

"In fact, she usually surprises you with her awesomeness," Marcus observed.

It was nice to see Marcus looking a bit more upbeat these days. Zoey had hated seeing him so mopey over Allie.

"True," Zoey said. "I guess I'll just wait and see."

She didn't have to wait very long. Zoey was late for the bus the next morning, so she didn't have time to check the latest developments on the auction page. At school, Libby met her and Kate when they got off the bus.

"Have you seen the auction page?" she exclaimed, practically jumping up and down with excitement.

"No. What's going on?" Kate asked.

"Daphne Shaw posted a shout-out about it on her blog," Libby said, "and the bids are going wild! We're getting close to the goal!"

Zoey smiled. She should have known her fashion fairy godmother wouldn't let her down.

It turned out that Daphne had even done a step better. She left a comment on Zoey's blog saying that she'd sent tips to several fashion news sites, and they'd all linked to Daphne's blog post about the auction. By lunchtime, the hits on the auction page were going through the roof!

"How much is it at now?" Priti asked. "I'm so excited I can barely eat my lunch!"

"Four hundred dollars!" Libby exclaimed. "Wait, another bid! Four hundred and ten!"

"And it's not even Friday yet!" Kate said.

"This is so great! I bet you'll have enough for

the refrigerator if this keeps up," Zoey said.

"I hope so!" Libby said. "It's awesome—and all thanks to Daphne."

That wasn't the end of Daphne's awesomeness. When Zoey got home from school that day, there was a package from Daphne's studio. Inside was one of Daphne's dresses and a note:

Dear Zoey,

I'm sending this as a Bat Mitzvah present for your wonderful friend Libby, who has been so generous with her time—and with her beloved Sew Zoey Bat Mitzvah dress. She sure knows how to give back, and I hope that more kids will learn from her example. Libby is fortunate to have a friend like you supporting her in her efforts.

Your friend,
Daphne Shaw

P.S. If it's not the right size, let my assistant know Libby's correct one, and we'll exchange.

Libby was thrilled with the gift. "That's so nice of her!" she said.

"Try it on to see if it fits," Zoey suggested. "Then I can take a picture of you wearing it to send to her."

Daphne didn't usually design clothes for tweens, but she'd made Libby a beautiful lavender A-line dress with a scattered floral print. It fit her pretty well considering Daphne had never met Libby and didn't know her size.

"I love it," Libby said. "I *am* sad to give up my Sew Zoey dress, but it will be worth it if we can get the fridge for the food pantry. And now it's doubly worth it!"

"Maybe good things came to you because you were doing good things," Zoey observed. "You know, what goes around comes around, or whatever."

"I don't know if that's what happened," Libby said. "But as long as we've raised enough to get the fridge for the food pantry, I'm happy!"

The girls made plans to be together for the final hour of bidding after school on Friday. They gathered around the computer at Libby's house, and together with Mrs. Flynn and Sophie, they watched the screen as a bidding war picked up and the minutes ticked down.

"Can you believe this?" Libby asked.

"I know, it's crazy!" Kate exclaimed. "It's like a feeding frenzy!"

"Look!" Priti said. "It's almost up to six hundred dollars!"

"Now it's six fifty!" Zoey said. She couldn't believe someone was willing to pay that much money for a dress made by . . . her!

They all counted down the final ten seconds. "Ten, nine, eight, seven, six, five, four, three . . . two . . . ONE!"

The final bid, which came in right at the last minute, was for seven hundred dollars!

The girls danced excitedly around the room.

Libby checked the computer again, as if she almost couldn't believe it was real.

"Oh look! I just got a message from the top bidder through the site," Libby said. "It turns out she works with Daphne Shaw!" She started to read the message aloud. "'We've been looking for a Bat Mitzvah dress for my daughter, Becky. Her theme is 'Becky in Bloom,' so the floral theme of this dress fits perfectly. Would you be able to send it overnight so we have time for alterations? I will, of course, pay extra for that. Good luck with the project, and congratulations on your Bat Mitzvah.' Isn't that cool?"

"I've already had the dress dry-cleaned and packed up in a box, so we can send it to her tomorrow morning," Mrs. Flynn said.

"So do you have enough?" Zoey asked.

"I'm one hundred and fifty dollars short," Libby said.

"Listen, honey, Dad and I spoke about this last night. We agreed that we'd donate the last bit you need, because you've worked so hard to make this happen, and we're very proud of you," Mrs. Flynn said.

Libby hugged her mom. "Thank you!" she said. "I love you!"

"How does it feel?" Kate asked. "You've worked so hard for this."

"It feels good!" Libby said. "I can't wait to tell the director of the food pantry we actually did it!"

On Sunday morning, as Zoey was eating her pancakes, Libby called.

"I talked to the food pantry's director, and he's arranged for a photographer from the local paper to come on Tuesday after school to do a story about me raising the money for the fridge. I want you to come too because it was your idea to auction the dress—and Daphne putting it on her blog made all the difference."

"I was just happy to help, but sure, I'll come," Zoey said.

"Great!" Libby said. "Mom will pick us up after school."

Zoey got off the phone and told her dad and Marcus about the photo opportunity.

"That's awesome," Marcus said. "But now it's time for the really important stuff. What do you think I used for the secret ingredient in the pancakes?"

The Webbers had a ritual of having Sunday morning pancakes, and they took turns making them with an additional secret ingredient that the others had to guess.

"I'm not sure what you used. Maybe walnuts?" Zoey asked, "But I'm definitely tasting satisfaction, too."

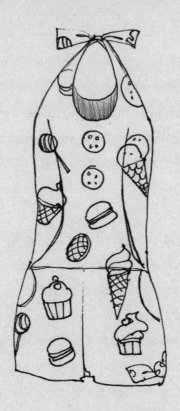

---------- CHAPTER 10 ----------

Sweets to the Sweet

It's really "sweet" to meet our fund-raising goal for the food pantry's new fridge. Thanks, Daphne Shaw, for the shout-out on your blog—traffic to the auction went through the roof! Especially sweet wishes to everyone who bid for the dress. I know the food pantry's patrons will really enjoy having fresh produce instead of just canned and packaged goods—and they'll appreciate eating healthier, too. But since I have a sweet tooth, this is inspired by sweets instead of vegetables. Sorry, Dr. Dryer (my dentist)! And sorry, Dad!

"Hi, Zoey!" Sophie called out as Mrs. Flynn's car pulled up in front of Mapleton Prep on Tuesday afternoon. "Can you sit next to me?"

"Sure." Zoey laughed.

Libby was wearing her Daphne Shaw dress, and Zoey wore the name tag dress she'd made. Kate joined them too because she was volunteering at the shelter and had arranged to carpool.

"I like your headband, Kate," Sophie said.

"Zoey made it for me," Kate said. "I'm trying to soften my look a little, without changing it completely."

"It suits you," Mrs. Flynn said. "Very pretty."

"How is it going with you and Tyler?" Libby asked.

"He's being more considerate of my feelings

since I talked to him at your Bat Mitzvah," Kate explained to her friends. "But I figured I'd try a few new things, too, as long as I still feel comfortable with them."

"It's like having the best of both worlds," Zoey said. "I'm glad I could actually help this time instead of messing things up!"

When they arrived at the food pantry, Kate and Zoey helped Libby take a huge check from the back of the car.

"It seems ridiculous to have this big check, but the food pantry's manager said I should order one so it would make more of an impact in the photos than handing them a regular check," Mrs. Flynn explained.

"Can they actually deposit this?" Zoey asked. "Imagine going up to the bank teller with it!"

"Or trying to put it in the ATM!" Kate said, giggling.

"No! This is just for the pictures," Libby said. "Mom has a regular check for depositing."

"Let me help carry it too!" Sophie begged.

Kate gave up her spot so Sophie could help carry the enormous check. Sophie was tall for her age but could still barely see above it.

"I've got to go meet Tyler to start my volunteer shift, anyway," she said. "Have fun with the paparazzi!"

Inside, the food pantry's manager, Mrs. Reed, waited with the director, board members, and a reporter and photographer from the local paper. They all congratulated Libby on her hard work and thanked her for making such an important gift to the organization.

"I wish I had more people with your energy on the board!" the director said. "We'd raise enough money to double the size of the building in no time!"

The reporter interviewed Libby, asking her why she'd chosen the food pantry as her mitzvah project and how she'd raised the money to buy the fridge.

"We held a bake sale, and I used some of the money I got as Bat Mitzvah gifts, and finally I auctioned off the dress that my friend Zoey designed and made for me," Libby explained. "She writes the blog Sew Zoey."

"Oh, so you're Zoey Webber!" exclaimed the reporter, turning to Zoey.

Zoey pointed to the Zoey name tag on her dress. "That's me!"

"I've been wanting to approach you about doing a human interest piece about our local design star," the reporter said.

"Um . . . sure," Zoey said. "That would be cool."

Mrs. Reed came over and asked if they were almost done with the interview. "I'd like to make a short speech, and then we can do the formal presentation of the check," she said.

"That works for me," the reporter said. He signaled to the photographer, who arranged everyone where he wanted them to stand so the lighting was optimal.

"I'd like to thank you all for coming today," Mrs. Reed started off. "We've had big donations before, but this is the first time one has come from a middle school student, which makes it all the more special."

As she went on about how grateful the food pantry was, Zoey looked around the room at town residents picking up their boxes of food. Then she caught a glimpse of a shocked, pale, familiar face, and gasped under her breath. *Is that . . . Ivy?* Zoey wondered, then saw that it was.

Ivy turned her head away quickly, as if she didn't want Zoey to see her. What was she doing here? Zoey was pretty sure she wasn't a volunteer, since Ivy volunteered at the retirement home.

Zoey couldn't investigate because it was time for photographs, and when she looked that way again, Ivy had disappeared.

As soon as the photographer finished, Zoey said, "I'll be back in a minute" to Libby, and went to search for Ivy. She finally found her in the parking lot, waiting for her mother.

"Hey, Ivy," Zoey said. "I was surprised to see you here."

"I'll bet," Ivy said. "You're probably going to tell everyone now."

"Tell everyone what?"

Ivy stared down at the ground and kicked a pebble with her shoe. "That I was here with Mom getting food."

"*That's* why you were here?" Zoey asked. "But . . . *why*?"

"My dad lost his job a few months ago," Ivy said. "Mom works, but . . . well, what she earns isn't enough to support the whole family, so . . . we have to come here to get help to make ends meet. I usually wait in the car."

"I'm so sorry," Zoey said. "That must be really hard for all of you."

"It is," Ivy admitted. "Really hard. It stinks. But listen, Zoey, please—"

"What?"

"You can't tell Emily. Please, promise me whatever you do, you won't tell anyone, but especially not Emily."

Ivy's eyes pleaded with Zoey to make the promise.

Zoey thought about how, not so long ago, Ivy demanded that her friends buy designer bags and shoes in order to fit in, and Zoey realized it must be such a turnaround for her to be the one who couldn't afford to buy things. She wondered if Ivy's sudden change in fortune had anything to do with her becoming nicer recently. Maybe struggling to make ends meet had made her less superficial, or at least made her understand other people better.

"It's okay, Ivy. Your secret is safe with me," she said. "I don't think Libby and Kate saw you."

Ivy breathed a visible sigh of relief.

"Thanks, Zoey. I'm really . . . "

Zoey didn't find out what she was, because just then Ivy's mom came out of the building with a box of groceries. Ivy said a quick, "Um . . . bye," and walked away.

The next day in industrial arts, Ivy showed no sign of having seen Zoey at the food pantry the day before. She walked in with Emily, as usual, and didn't even acknowledge Zoey or Priti, who were sitting at the workbench opposite her.

"Oh! Did you see my latest addition?" Emily said, extending her wrist to show off yet another woven bracelet. "I think this one is my absolute favorite. Although there's another one at the store I liked too. I might have to go back and get it."

"Wow. That's really pretty," Ivy said. "I love the purple and pink together, and the little hearts."

"Where's yours?" Emily demanded. "I thought you said you were going to get one."

"Oh . . . I . . ."

Zoey watched Ivy's neck and face flush as she tried to come up with another excuse for why she hadn't bought one of the woven bracelets. Now Zoey knew that Ivy really had a good excuse for not getting one, even though she shouldn't have had to explain at all. She wished Ivy could just tell Emily that bracelets weren't high on her priority list because of what was going on with her family. But as she'd learned from trying to help her former best friend, Shannon, who'd been hard-pressed to keep up with Ivy's fashion demands, it just wasn't going to happen.

"My mom has had to work late a lot recently, so she hasn't been able to take me to the store to get them," Ivy said. "But . . . I'm planning to get one as soon as she can take me."

"Your mom should buy you two for making you wait so long to get one," Emily said.

Ivy gave a fake laugh that almost sounded to Zoey liked a choked sob.

"Totally," she agreed.

She sounded like she was barely holding it together. How come Emily couldn't see that? *Maybe people just see what they want to see,* Zoey thought. *Or they're blind.*

How long would Ivy be able to keep up appearances, pretending that nothing had changed?

CHAPTER 11

Lifting the Veil

It's funny how you think you know everything about a person, but then you learn something that makes you realize that maybe all you've been seeing is the veil they've been wearing to cover up their true feelings. Suddenly, you think: Wow, maybe I didn't know that person so well at all. It makes you realize that people have all kinds of reasons for acting the way they do, and maybe we shouldn't always be so quick to judge.

I'd love to have a chance to wear a hat like one of these somewhere—maybe I should move to England. Mrs. Holbrooke had a whole bunch of fancy hats we borrowed for Hat Day during Spirit Week a while back, because apparently they wear hats a lot more over there. It's a shame, because they're so much fun to design— and to wear. A great hat really "tops off" an outfit, don't you think? Here are some I came up with, just for fun!

Zoey couldn't stop thinking about Ivy's dilemma. She knew Emily would keep asking about the bracelets, and Ivy would have to keep thinking of excuses why she didn't have one yet. Even though Ivy had made her life miserable for a long time, she'd been nicer to Zoey recently, and Zoey didn't like to see anyone going through a hard time. It must be really difficult to have to worry about having enough to eat. She was glad that Dad had a job and that there was always food in the fridge. Okay, so maybe sometimes they ran out of something, but then they put it on the shopping list for Dad to pick up the next time he went to the supermarket, and then it appeared again. What would it be like if Dad lost his job? She didn't even want to think about it.

She had to help Ivy somehow. But how?

She decided to check her blog for comments. Her Sew Zoey community always made her feel better—and they often inspired her with good ideas too.

There was a comment on her "Sweets to the Sweet" post from FashionsistaNYC, a.k.a. her mentor, Daphne Shaw.

I was more than happy to give Libby's auction a shout-out on my blog, and I'm thrilled that in doing so, she was able to raise enough money for the food pantry's refrigerator. I've been fortunate to have been helped by so many people in my life that I'm a big believer in "paying it forward." Well done!

Paying it forward . . . , Zoey repeated to herself. Suddenly, she had an idea of how *she* could pay it forward—for Ivy! She did some research online, then went down the hallway to her brother's room.

"Marcus? Can you drive me to A Stitch in Time? Like, now?"

"Sure," Marcus said. "What's the rush?"

"I want to make something, and I need to get some materials."

"Thanks for being so specific," Marcus said. "But since I'm a good brother, I'll just go grab the car keys."

In the car, Marcus turned up the radio and started singing. Zoey realized it was the most cheerful she'd seen him since Allie had broken up with him.

"How are you doing?" she asked. "Are you feeling better about . . . you know, *stuff*?"

Marcus laughed.

"*Stuff*? You mean like Allie?" he asked.

"Yeah, like Allie," Zoey said.

"I'm still upset about the breakup," Marcus confessed. "But now that I've had more time to think about it, I realized that . . . we'd kind of been on different pages lately, if you know what I mean. We're both busy with different things—me with my band and her with her accessories line and her blog—so we weren't spending as much time together, and then when we did, it seemed like we argued a lot."

"But you still seemed happy together, I thought."

"I still like Allie . . . a lot," Marcus said. "But I also realized that she gets really freaked out about stuff that doesn't seem like such a big deal to me."

"Like what?" Zoey asked.

"Remember the time at the pet shelter when the dog jumped in a puddle and got mud on her new blouse?" Marcus asked.

"Yeah!" Zoey said. "How could I forget?"

"So I guess maybe I'm just too laid back to go out with someone like Allie, who can be a bit dramatic. Maybe I need to date someone who's a little more . . . I don't know . . . *low key*."

"Or maybe Libby was right," Zoey said. "Maybe dog people should just date dog people, and cat people should just date cat people."

Marcus laughed. "I'll make sure to give any future girlfriend candidates a pet survey before going out with them."

Zoey was glad to hear that Marcus seemed to be moving on, especially since Allie already seemed to be pretty involved with her new boyfriend, Oliver. At least Zoey wouldn't feel like she was betraying Marcus if she still remained friends with Allie, which she still wanted to do, or at least work toward—after all, they'd started out as friends, and Allie was the only one who understood what it was like to be a young fashion designer.

Walking into A Stitch in Time was like entering a second home—especially when Zoey was greeted by the owner, Jan.

"Zoey! What an unexpected pleasure!" Jan said, coming out from behind the counter to give Zoey a hug. "How can I help you today? What exciting project are you working on now?"

"It's a paying-it-forward project," Zoey said.

She showed Jan the pictures she'd printed from the Internet, then explained what she wanted to do.

"Which kind of thread do you think will be the best to use?" she asked. "And I'll need some kind of clasp as well. One that looks as close to the one in the picture as possible."

"No problem, my dear," Jan said. "I've got every-thing you need."

When they'd gathered all the materials, Jan gave Zoey an even bigger discount than she usually did.

"Consider it my way of being part of the paying-it-forward project," she said.

"Thanks, Jan!" Zoey said. "I'll let you know how it goes!"

Zoey spent that evening working on her project, trying to make it as close to the picture as she possibly could, and she was really pleased with the finished product. The next day, she made sure she got to industrial arts class early, before anyone else arrived, and she put a little box on Ivy's stool. Then she got busy working on her latest shop project—a wooden football sculpture for her dad.

"Hi, Zoey," Priti said when she got to class. "The football is starting to take shape. It doesn't look like a watermelon anymore!"

Zoey laughed. "Mr. Weldon showed me how to plane down the ends to make them more pointy and football-like."

When Ivy arrived, she found the box on her stool and looked around, curious. Zoey pretended to mind her own business, intent on her project. But from the corner of her eye she watched Ivy open the box and read the note, which said "I hope you like this! From, a friend," and then saw Ivy pull out the woven bracelet that Zoey had made for her and gasp in surprised delight. It looked just like the kind Emily had been bragging about for weeks.

Ivy put it on her wrist immediately, holding it out and admiring it.

"That's really cute," Priti said.

"Thanks," Ivy said. "I think it's a surprise gift from Emily. She loves these bracelets."

Just then Emily walked in, and Ivy's attention turned to her immediately.

"Look," she said, showing off her bracelet to Emily. "It's perfect!"

"Nice," Emily said. "I didn't see that one at the store. It's about time you finally got one."

Ivy looked confused. Emily's comment made it clear she hadn't given her the bracelet. Ivy glanced around the room as if she was trying to figure out who did. When Ivy spotted Zoey, she gave her a questioning look, as if to ask, *Was it you?*

Zoey had wanted to give Ivy the bracelet anonymously, so people wouldn't ask questions that might expose Ivy's situation. But Ivy seemed to want to know, so Zoey gave the slightest nod, small enough that Priti didn't notice it.

Ivy's eyes widened.

"So, which colors are you getting next?" Emily pushed. "You should have bought more. You really need a few to get the look."

"Um, I don't know," Ivy told Emily.

Later, as they worked on their projects, Zoey glanced up to see Ivy staring at her, with a strange expression on her face.

Zoey smiled. To her surprise, Ivy smiled back.

Zoey knew that it wouldn't be long before Emily found something else that Ivy just *had* to buy. But at least she'd helped Ivy out for now.

"I'm starving," Marcus said. "I hope Aunt Lulu made pancakes."

"Uncle John likes to cook," Dad said as he rang

the doorbell. "I'm sure you won't leave hungry."

Buttons greeted them with licks and a furiously wagging tail as soon as the door opened.

"Come on in," Uncle John said. "Lulu's in the kitchen. Your Sunday brunch awaits."

"I can't wait," Zoey said, picking up Buttons and cuddling her. "Aunt Lulu makes really good brunch."

"She has something special planned for dessert," Uncle John said. "But don't tell her I told you, or I'm a dead man!"

All through brunch, Zoey wondered about the special dessert—after all, she did have kind of a sweet tooth, and it was getting sweeter after all the treats at Libby's Bat Mitzvah.

"Okay, everyone ready for dessert?" Aunt Lulu asked.

"Yes!" Zoey exclaimed. "I'm always ready for dessert."

"That's my girl," Dad said.

"Just like your mom too," Aunt Lulu said, smiling. She went to the dining room and came back with a covered tray. "So, John and I invited you over for brunch today because we wanted to see you, but also because we have some exciting news. . . ."

She took the cover off the tray to reveal mini cupcakes with yellow icing and baby motifs.

"Wait . . . does this mean . . . you're having a BABY?" Marcus said.

Uncle John put his arm around Aunt Lulu. "We are! You're going to have a new cousin."

Marcus, Zoey, and their dad jumped up from their seats, talking and hugging and yippeeing with joy. Buttons started barking, confused by all the hubbub, and Uncle John patted her head to let her know everything was okay. Everything was better than okay—it was great! Finally, eager to get more information, they all sat back down.

"Wow! That's so exciting!" Zoey said. "Do you know if it's a boy or a girl?"

"Not yet," Aunt Lulu said. "We'll be happy with a healthy baby."

"It'll be fun to welcome a new member of the family, won't it, kids?" Dad said.

"Yes—and just think of all the great baby clothes I can design!" Zoey exclaimed.

As they all enjoyed the cupcakes, Zoey thought

about how much fun it would be to have a baby cousin. She wondered if her little cousin would like sewing. It would be so much fun to teach him or her how to make clothes.

Her aunt and uncle's news meant exciting changes for the family, and also for Sew Zoey. With all the bibs, onesies, and bonnets Zoey planned to make, her future cousin would be the best-dressed baby in town!

Zoey is getting gifty!

Be sure to check out the next
book in the Sew Zoey series:

SEWING in
CIRCLES

Great stories are like great accessories: You can never have too many! Collect all the books in the Sew Zoey series:

Ready to Wear

On Pins and Needles

Lights, Camera, Fashion!

Stitches and Stones

Cute as a Button

A Tangled Thread

Knot Too Shabby!

Swatch Out!

A Change of Lace

Bursting at the Seam

Clothes Minded

Dressed to Frill

Sewing in Circles